Nicole

by

Simone Poirier-Bures

Pottersfield Press
Lawrencetown Beach, Nova Scotia, Canada

Copyright © 2000 Simone Poirier-Bures

All rights reserved. No part of this publication may be reproduced or transmitted in any form or by any means, electronic or mechanical, including photocopying, or by any information storage or retrieval system, without permission in writing from the publisher.

Canadian Cataloguing in Publication Data
    Poirier-Bures, Simone
      Nicole
ISBN 1-895900-34-4
I. Title
PS8581.0235N53 2000   C813'.54   C00-950127-4
PR9199.3.P558N53 2000

Back cover photo: John McCormick

Pottersfield Press gratefully acknowledges the ongoing support of the Nova Scotia Department of Tourism and Culture, Cultural Affairs Division, as well as The Canada Council for the Arts. We acknowledge the financial support of the Government of Canada through the Book Publishing Industry Development Program for our publishing activities.

Printed in Canada

Pottersfield Press
83 Leslie Road
East Lawrencetown
Nova Scotia, Canada, B2Z 1P8
To order: telephone toll-free 1-800-NIMBUS9 (1-800-646-2879)

for my sister Jeannette,
and for Joanne, friend of my youth

Acknowledgements

All except one of these pieces were originally published (sometimes in slightly different form) in the following periodicals and anthologies: "Searching for Dad" in *Weber Studies*; "Danger Water" in *The Florida Review*; "Ten" in *Two Worlds Walking* (New Rivers Press, 1994); "She Wouldn't Want Them" in *Artemis XI*; "Will Someone Tell Me, Please" in *Emrys Journal*; "Nothing Ever happens" in *Potato Eyes*; "What They Knew" in *Moving Out*; "Circle of Light" in *Artemis XIV*; "Return" in *The Virgina Quarterly Review*.

Special thanks to Pascal Poirier, Jeannette Poirier, and Sister Isobel Page, who helped track down some of the photographs for this book; and to Dimity Purvis, who supplied the photo of the prefabs. Thanks to the Public Archives of Nova Scotia for permission to use the photo of the Green Lantern soda shop (Bollinger Collection 1941-229), and to the Nova Scotia Museum History Collection for permission to use the two photos of Barrington Street by E.G.L. Wetmore.

Un grand merci to Sally Ross for her sharp editor's eye, to Gyorgyi Voros for her support and advice, and to George Elliott Clarke. Above all, my special gratitude to Allen, who makes everything possible.

Contents

Writing From Life   7

Part 1

Searching for Dad   15

Danger Water   25

Ten   37

She Wouldn't Want Them   47

Will Someone Tell Me, Please?   60

Nothing Ever Happens   73

What They Knew   89

Circle of Light   107

Evangeline   112

Part 2

Return   127

Writing From Life

Anyone reading these stories who knows me will recognize the similarities between my own background and that of Nicole: the family of two boys and two girls, the older father, the Acadian heritage, the basement full of penny candy. Like Nicole, I, too, grew up in Halifax in the 1950s, went to Convent School, and left the province to attend university in the United States. Is Nicole, then, really me? Are her stories simply my stories, disguised? If so, why pass them off as fiction, rather than acknowledge them as memoir?

The answer is that Nicole is both me and not me. She is a persona, a vehicle for both memory and imagination.

I began writing these stories in the mid-1980s, after a visit to Halifax (described in "Return," following the stories) had churned up decades-old memories. The

Halifax I remembered, the Halifax of the 1950s, had shape-shifted, disappeared. The old had been swallowed up by the new. Yet the old continued to haunt me. Ghost ponds and ghost woods lurked beneath certain parking lots and shopping centers; ghost trolleys still clattered along the streets. For me, the Halifax of the 1950s was an enchanted time, the city full of small wonders; the witnessing, remembering, "I" could not let it go.

My first impulse was to record, to preserve it all in a memoir. So I began writing down everything I could recall from my earliest childhood onward — the stories my mother told about her teaching days in the French parts of Nova Scotia; the mystery surrounding my father's life before us; the trips to the country to visit my French-speaking relatives. The more I wrote, the more I remembered; it was like dipping into a magic well that refilled as I emptied it. I was aware, of course, of the shifting, selectiveness of memory, its notorious unreliability. But how joyful it was, this process of reclaiming, this bringing to light of half-forgotten things!

After I had completed about sixty pages, I sat down to read what I had written and discovered a hard truth: my "memoir" was far too fragmented to appeal to anyone but myself and my family. It needed structure and drama; it needed *story*.

What is "story" but a series of connected events, where one thing leads to another, with cause and effect? We can make story out of anything if we select and arrange enough, invent a few details. The "lies" of fiction. So I began carving patterns out of that huge sea of memory, arranging and rearranging the bits. Memory, given free rein, will always yield to imagination. Its impulse is to find connection, to make story, for that is how we make meaning out of our lives. Nicole became a handy vehicle, this girl who is both me and not me.

Did I get to be Evangeline on a float during the Acadian festival of 1955, the bicentennial of the Great Deportation, as Nicole does, in "Ten"? Did we all dress up in Acadian costumes for the parade? And the huge pans of *pâté à la râpure,* the decorated oxen, the teary-eyed elderly people lining the highway — did it all happen? Does it matter? I grew up hearing stories of Evangeline and the Acadian expulsion; my mother, who was a great story-teller, made sure we never forgot. At some point, the story of Evangeline struck me as the most romantic and tragic story I'd ever heard. Was I ten? I'm not sure. But I do remember the feeling of my tenth year. The world seemed full of passion and beauty; and I became aware of love, and myself as female, at the same time. That year, anything seemed possible. I had not yet learned the limitations placed on girls and women; instead, the whole wide world seemed to lay itself at my ten-year-old feet.

As in "Danger Water," there was a stolen ring in my own life. Thieves regularly broke into our basement, and every winter, we all skated on the pond by St. Patrick's Home. And there was indeed a boy who stole from my father's truck, whose mother dragged him to our front door to make restitution. But did all this happen in one winter, as it does in the story? I have no idea. What is "true" here, is that one winter, I saw the connection between my stealing a ring and what was happening in our basement. I learned the meaning of "thief," saw the human face behind the word, and recognized myself there.

In these stories, then, imagination supplied the connective tissue; memory, the raw material. And while the stories describe many of my own important passages, they are as *Nicole* experienced them; Nicole, my imagined, constructed, self.

In "Searching For Dad," Nicole tries to learn something about her silent father who has only "one story"; in "Danger Water," as I have already mentioned, she identifies with a young thief who steals from her father's truck; in "Ten," she discovers a romantic heroine, a model for womanhood, and her own identity as an Acadian. In "She Wouldn't Want Them," she finds that a basement full of candy is not equally valued by everyone, and so learns something about class and position. In two of the stories, "Will Someone Tell Me, Please" and "What They Knew," Nicole struggles to uncover the facts of life, and what it means to be a woman in a time when the expectations for women were less than they are now. Finally, in "Evangeline," Nicole reaffirms her Acadian heritage, and follows the path of many of her ancestors.

Some of the stories are told in first person, some in third; some are in past tense, some in present. How I chose to tell each story depended largely on my relationship to the material, how intimately remembered it was, how much interpreted or invented.

At the same time that I was writing about Nicole, I began envisioning a work about the whole family, not just Nicole — one in which the mother and father's story would also be told. This was to become my novel, *Candyman*. Those who have read it will find many of the same characters here. I borrowed a few bits from these stories to construct a coherent world for the novel, and went on from there.

But Nicole had her own life, apart from what is told in *Candyman*. As in hypertext novels and certain video games where the reader/player can follow a character into a different story line, and then later (or not) reconnect to another part of the story, Nicole had her own adventures, her own secret life, apart from her family's. This is what is told here.

The stories and the novel, then, are parts of the same whole, a whole that does not exist as a fixed reality, but like the past, keeps shapeshifting, reinventing itself. Now that I have written about them, my old memories are no longer intact; imagination has swallowed them up, made them something new. That is the price of writing from experience. Yet these stories, with their inventions, their little "lies," somehow manage to do what memory alone could not: they tell the truth of what it was like to grow up in the Halifax of the 1950s and early 1960s, to be a candyman's daughter, to be an Acadian, to be a young woman — at that time, in that place.

Part 1

Searching For Dad

There are clues in the kitchen cupboards: a cobalt blue cheese dish, four crystal goblets with worn, gold leaf trim, a sculpted soup tureen, a white porcelain dish, a platter decorated with gold, rose, and green paint. They are abruptly unlike our pink and turquoise melmac plates and bowls, our plastic tumblers, our jelly jar glasses.

"They came from your father's house," my mother tells me. Your father's father and his father before that were captains of clipper ships. They brought home all those beautiful things when your father was a boy."

On Sundays at noon, the big platter with gold, rose, and green trim holds our roast chicken, or roast beef, or once in a great while, roast pork. The white porcelain dish holds the mashed potatoes or mashed turnips or yellow waxed beans. There was a glass pitcher once, that looked like it was made of diamonds, but we broke it making Kool-Aid.

On Sundays at noon, mountains of dishes appear on the counter for Annette to wash and me to dry. I turn the platter over in my towel. "Could this be from China?" I ask my mother.

"I don't know," she says.

"Isn't china supposed to come from China?"

"Some of it does," she says. "But those good dishes could have come from England or France or Belgium. Your grandfather used to go all over. I don't know if he ever went to China."

I run my thumb over the gold trim, thinking of China.

"All that happened a long time ago," my mother says. "Ask your father."

But when the dishes are all washed and dried and put away my father is having his nap. And when he wakes up I am down the street, or in my room reading.

My mother tells us that when she was five her father had tuberculosis and came home from the sanitarium to die. "He called all five of us children to his bedside, one by one," she says, "to say goodbye. He told me to obey my mother and to watch over my little sister. Then he kissed me for the last time."

My mother tells us about the general store my grandmother ran. "Getting an orange in your Christmas stocking was a special treat then," she says. "Jim, the hired man who helped run the farm, sometimes pretended to be Père Nöel and took my sisters and me for rides on his back."

"What was it like when *you* were a boy?" I ask my father. I am vaguely aware that he was a boy long before my mother was even born. But it is hard to count back that far, it is time unimaginable. "What was it like?" I ask. "Oh, like any boy's life, I suppose," he says, and goes back to his newspaper.

My mother tells us how they prepared for winter along Saint Mary's Bay. How they gathered carrots and potatoes and turnips and squash and apples to bury in fresh sawdust in deep bins in the cellar. "Once, when I was six," she says, blushing with remembered shame, "I gathered the fallen apples in my bloomers thinking I was being a big help. But everyone laughed at me and fed the apples to the pig."

When my mother talks about her girlhood, her eyes widen, her voice goes up a pitch or two. The girl's face shines out, from behind her own.

With my father, it is different. From him, there is only one story. In the winter when we go skating on the lake in Waverley, my father tells us about the ice floes that used to form in the harbors of Isle Madame, in Cape Breton, where he grew up. Once, ignoring all warnings, he ventured out too far on the ice. "I was ten," he says, "and thought I knew everything." He tells us how the part he was standing on broke off, how he watched, terrified, as the strip of dark water between himself and the shore widened. "Only by leaping from one chunk of ice to another was I able to reach safety," he says. He points to the frozen lake. "Be careful; it would be a terrible death."

We know this is a cautionary tale, meant to illustrate the folly of youth and the wisdom of parental advice. He tells this story every winter. But I listen anyway. I strain to picture this boy who lived so long ago, this boy who became my father, this boy with only one story. I search my father's balding head, his barrel-shaped body, his red neck with the loose skin for signs of the boy. I do not find him.

My mother tells us about the one-room schoolhouses she taught in throughout Nova Scotia before she met my father, the tiny villages where there was nothing to do, how she and a friend would walk ten miles on a Saturday night just to go to a dance.

My mother tells us how they travelled by sled sometimes, and heated bricks to put by their feet and wrapped horse and buffalo blankets around their legs to keep warm. How once she wore a tam cocked over her right ear because it was stylish and got frost bite in her left one.

"What did you do before you met Mom?" I want to ask my father. But he is reading his newspaper, or listening to a program on the radio, and I am playing Monopoly, or I just forget.

In the basement, a large leather suitcase encircled by two thick leather straps holds a brown greatcoat with large shiny buttons up and down the front, a metal helmet, a pair of binoculars, a fitted jacket with more buttons and a small stand-up collar. Annette and André and Claude and I take turns wearing the helmet and jacket when we play war, and spy on each other with

the binoculars. The greatcoat is so big and heavy we can hardly lift it.

"What did you do in the war?" we ask our father. We are vaguely aware that his was a different war than the one we know about from all the movies, the one that Mr. Penny across the street lost a finger in. But we are hungry for heroics so it doesn't matter. "I was a nurse in France," he says, not looking up from his newspaper. "Did you ever kill any bad guys?" we ask, "Or save any good guys?" "I don't believe in killing," he says. "We saved all we could." The corners of his mouth twitch a little as he talks, and he doesn't put down his paper, so we don't ask any more questions.

In the basement, Annette says: "He couldn't have been a nurse. Only girls are nurses." "Yeah," André says, "And nurses don't need helmets. And what about the binoculars? What would a nurse do with binoculars?" "Maybe he was a spy," someone suggests. "A good spy! And he has to keep it a secret forever because the bad guys might try to hurt us if they ever found out." We grow silent thinking of our father's heroic deeds, deeds for which he will never receive his proper glory, all because of us.

One Sunday morning, while rooting through the drawer above the glass bookcase looking for a lost bracelet, I find a small velvet box, dark blue, worn around the edges. Inside: a medal. I show it to Annette as she buttons her dress for Mass.

"See," she says, "I knew it all along."

My mother sits at the vanity powdering her nose. "What was it for?" we ask her.

"I'm sure it's nothing," she says, her red mouth curling. "They probably gave one to everyone who served."

When my father and André come home from early Mass we meet him at the door with the medal, gleaming from its case. My father takes off his brown Sunday hat and takes a deep breath. His suit smells faintly of moth balls and dry cleaning fluid. "They thought it was the war to end all wars," he says, taking the medal from my hands. "War is a terrible thing."

In late summer, Annette and I sprawl on the back steps drawing a treasure map. A toffee tin with a picture of Queen Elizabeth and Prince Philip holds the treasure: a green rhinestone earring whose mate is lost, a string of clear glass beads, three pennies.

Claude hovers around us, touching the tin, the toothpicks, the saucer of lemon juice.

"Stop bothering us," Annette says, pushing him away. She waves a ruler that reads: Do Unto Others As You Would Have Others Do Unto You.

Claude moves over to the side of the steps and folds his arms. "I know where a *real* pirate's treasure is anyway," he says. "Not just a pretend one." His black hair and eyes are glossy, like a cat's.

"Sure you do," Annette says.

"I do! I do!" he says.

"You're just making it up." We turn back to our map, dip our toothpicks into the lemon juice.

"I'm *not* making it up!" Claude says, thumping into the house. He comes out holding a faded red cloth bag with a drawstring top. "See," he says, "A *real* pirate's treasure."

"Where did you get that?" Annette hisses.

"I found it, and it's mine." He holds the bag behind him and backs away.

Annette and I leap on him and wrestle the bag out of his soft, chubby hands. As we loosen the string, dozens of tarnished copper coins spill out. Some are the size of quarters, but thinner. Others are as small as dimes.

"They're mine," Claude says, watching the coins as we finger them. Some of the figures and letters are worn smooth; on others we can still distinguish numbers: 1854, 1890, 1862, 1859.

"Where did you get them?" Annette demands. "Answer me!"

Claude hangs his head. "In Dad's bottom drawer."

Annette and I look at each other. A little shiver runs down my spine.

Hours later, when we hear the truck, Annette and I bolt to the basement. Cradled in my hands is the small, heavy bag. My father climbs out of the truck and squints at us from behind his wire-rimmed glasses. "What's the matter?"

I hold the bag up like an offering.

"That's my penny collection," he says, taking off his cap. "I haven't seen it in a long time. Where did you find it?"

"How can they be pennies?" we ask. "They're too big."

My father closes the big wooden basement doors and lifts the iron bar into place. "Coins used to be different," he says. "Before Confederation, every province made its own coins."

We follow him to the desk, our questions buzzing around him like sand flies.

"I started saving them when I was a boy," he says. "Some of those are from before I was born."

I tense to listen, hungry for his words. But he turns and starts up the stairs, moving his heavy body up, one step at a time.

"You'd better give those back to me," he says when we reach the top. "They might be valuable some day, and I don't want you losing them." I watch him go into the bedroom and pull out the bottom drawer of my mother's hope chest. When he comes out he says, "What's for supper?"

Evenings, when my father dozes in his arm chair, the news paper folded across his chest, I slip into the bedroom and take the red bag from its drawer. Fingering the smooth, cool coins, I try to imagine the boy who once owned them. He is ten, and his clothes are old-fashioned, like the ones I've seen in old movies. But I cannot see his face — he is too far away: he stands on an ice floe, staring at the shore.

Danger Water

"It's worse than last time," her father said.

Nicole stared at the violated boxes, the mini Tootsie Rolls and coconut balls scattered on the basement floor, the broken glass gleaming like ice. In their nightclothes, still smelling of sleep, they had all come down to the basement to see. Her father had pulled his pants on over his long johns; white stubble covered his cheeks. This in itself made every thing seem odd, as her father's face was usually smooth and pink by the time he called them in the morning. The cats, Clem and Solomon and Baby and her five kittens, came out of their hiding places and tiptoed through the rubble.

"They must have been looking for money, too," her mother said, pointing to the desk in the corner. They all turned to look at the gaping drawers, the scattered papers.

"*Maudit enfant bleu!*" her father said.

They all fell silent. It had to be bad for their father to curse in French. Claude picked up one of the mini Tootsie Rolls, unwrapped it, and popped it into his mouth.

"Don't do that!" Nicole said, poking him. "They need it for the evidence, don't they, Dad."

"I thought having a basement would put an end to this," he said. "How's a man supposed to make a living this way?"

Nicole remembered when her father had kept the candy in the shed outside: sometimes she would wake to her father's voice, angry, talking into the black phone that sat on the little table in her parents' bedroom. They would all get up and rush to the kitchen window to stare at the shed with its broken lock, the trail of penny candy spilling from the open door. She remembered her mother's white ankles, Claude's big toe sticking out of his red-footed pajamas, her father ferociously jabbing the fire in the kitchen stove with the long black poker. It was exciting, a little like Christmas morning, except that her mother was solemn, and her father angry.

But that was more than two years ago. After they got the basement everything was all right — until a few weeks ago. Then the trouble had started again.

"It's strange to think of them down here," her mother said. "Sneaking around while we were asleep. I didn't even hear anything." She put her arm around Claude.

"At least they didn't hurt the cats," Nicole said, picking up Clem and hugging him. Clem, with his half-chewed right ear and glossy orange coat, was her favourite.

"We need a watch dog," André said. "Like Lassie."

"Lassie's a collie dog and collies don't make good watch dogs," Annette said.

"They do too!" André yelled.

"We need *something* that's for sure," their father said in a tone that made them all fall silent again.

At breakfast, their mother said, "The thieves seem to be worse in autumn. It must be the long nights. They can hide in the dark and no one sees their evil deeds."

"I'd like to take those thieves and bash them," Claude said, slapping his cream of wheat with the back of his spoon.

"There's nothing worse than a thief," their mother continued. "People sneaking around taking things that belong to other people, things they work hard for."

"Could we get a dog, then, huh, Mom?" André asked.

"The last thing we need is something else to feed," she said. "But I suppose you can ask your father. Later." Their father was in the basement waiting for the police.

"We could get a boy dog and call him Laddie," André said. "I could make him a little bed."

"What about the cats?" Annette said. "Dogs and cats don't like each other, dummy."

"We could give the cats away."

"Not *our* cats!" Claude sputtered.

"Don't worry," Annette said. "Dad would never give away the cats, would he, Nicole."

The cats were at the side of the stove now, swarming over the bowl of milk and the plate of canned horse meat. Even with all the commotion, her father hadn't forgotten to feed them. But Nicole wasn't thinking of the cats just then. Her mother's words had stirred up something inside her, something vague and troubling.

By noon, all the kids in the neighborhood had heard of the new break-in. "Holy mackerel!" Gordie Smith said to everyone. "The LeBlancs had another thief in their basement."

After supper, the air around the lamppost where Nicole and Annette and their friends gathered crackled with rumor.

"They found a box, half of it gone, in the bushes up by Bayers Road," Wayne said.

"I heard it was *two* boxes," his brother Ducky corrected, "and there was stuff spilled all over. Some little kids who go to Edgewood School found it." Their eyes shone like hounds' eyes.

"Who could it be?" Nicole asked.

"I think Johnny Powers did it," Wayne said.

"More likely it was Jimmy Dunford," Gloria said.

"It couldn't have been him," Ducky countered. "He's already in St. Patrick's Home for starting a fire."

There were six of them tonight. Not enough for Red Rover, but enough for hide-and-seek. Though it was a perfect night for games — cool, crisp, and except for the streetlight, pitch dark — none of them felt like playing.

"Just think about it," Wayne said. "Johnny Powers had a pocketful of candy at recess and couldn't explain where he got it."

"I saw two of those big boys who live on Connaught Avenue staring at your father's truck," Ducky said. "Those tough boys who smoke and always pick on little kids. It could be them."

"They're all troublemakers," Annette said. "They all belong in the Home."

The little group all nodded and shifted from foot to foot. "Yeah, they should lock them all up!"

"And throw away the key!"

"Maybe it's not them," Annette said in a low voice. "Maybe it's a grown man, one of those bad men who offer kids candy and make them do things. Maybe that's what he wanted the candy for."

They all got very still. They'd heard about Jimmy Boutilier and what a strange man had made him do in the woods the summer before. No one was sure of the details, but everyone knew it involved pulling down his pants. Wayne poked at a pile of dead leaves with his foot. Nicole pulled her jacket close. Suddenly the world seemed full of badness. Bad boys breaking into basements and sheds and starting fires. Bad men doing bad things to children. Outside the small circle of light, Nicole could feel the darkness hovering. Behind the sheds and in the alleys and under the bushes at the end of the street, badness waited, lapping against them like a dark ocean.

That night, while Nicole slept, her house became an ark, dipping and listing dangerously on an angry, churning sea. Each time the ark-house dipped, the water edged closer to the two open windows in the corner of the bedroom. One strong wave, and a wall of water would come crashing into the room. Trapped in sleep, Nicole couldn't get up to close the windows, couldn't even call out for help, or to warn the others. Suddenly the great wave came. The room spun. Swirls of bright green and yellow and red and orange and blue water filled the room, sucking her under.

Nicole woke, swallowing air in big gulps, the sheets around her clammy. She sat up and peered toward the windows, astounded to see that they were closed, that the room was not spinning, and that they were all safe, Annette beside her, the boys in their bunks on the other side of the room. She lay back down. The darkness breathed like sleep. It moved with sound: little snuffling sounds from Claude, whose nose was always plugged, heavy gurgling sounds from the room next door where her father and mother slept. Annette shifted a little, nuzzled up to her. In the whole wide world, only she, Nicole, was awake. It was a nice feeling, in a way. A feeling of power. Then she remembered: this was the time when thieves were awake. She buried her head in her pillow.

Over the next few weeks, the detective came back to talk in a low voice to her father. But there were no clues, and no charges were made. Her father replaced the broken window and told André, "Stop pestering me about a damn dog." The children who gathered around the lamp post after supper resumed their games of Red Rover and Simon Says.

Nicole, meanwhile, dreamed of hands — tiny rubbery green hands. They surrounded her bed, swarmed out from underneath, hundreds of them, all wanting, grabbing, trying to grab *her*. Each night, before she got into bed, she leaned over and looked under it. She huddled as close to Annette as possible until she fell asleep. She didn't tell anyone about the dreams.

One afternoon, just before supper, Nicole heard a knock at the front door. A woman in an old coat and a stocky, red-faced boy around her own age stood on the front steps. They looked nervous and queer. She called her mother.

"I found Billy with these," the woman told Claire. The boy held out a large box of chocolate buds.

"He took them from your husband's truck last night while he was loading, didn't you Billy." She poked him ferociously with her elbow.

"Yes," came a small voice. The boy's head was bent so far over Nicole could hardly see his face. His brown jacket hung heavily on his shoulders.

"Well I'm here to pay for them," the woman said. Her voice was high and tight. "I'll not have a thief in my house." She took out a small, worn change purse and began counting out dimes and quarters into Claire's hand. Nicole stared at the top of the boy's head, at his blond-brown hair sticking out in spiky clumps. "Since you've paid for them, you might as well keep the rest," Claire said in a soft voice.

"No, you keep them," the woman returned, pulling her scarf more tightly around her head.

They watched the pair go up the street, the woman jerking the boy along beside her.

"Now that's a really good mother," Claire said. "If that boy doesn't end up in St. Patrick's Home it will be because of her."

Claire put the opened box of chocolate buds on the drop-leaf table in the living room. "You might as well eat these," she said. "Your father can't sell them now."

Claude and André each grabbed a big handful. "Boy, he must have wanted these a lot to *steal* them," André said.

"And *we* get to eat them!" Claude said. Claire gave him a sharp look.

"There are lots of things *I'd* like to have, but I'd never *steal*," Annette said. She plucked up one chocolate bud and popped it daintily into her mouth.

"His name was Billy," Nicole said suddenly.

They all looked at her.

"Do we know him?" Annette asked.

"I don't think so."

"What did he look like?" André asked. "I'd like to see what a thief looks like."

"He looked . . . I don't really remember," Nicole said. He had looked so ordinary. That was the trouble. He looked just like them. The word *thief* thudded against her heart like a stone.

Later, when no one was around, Nicole slipped into the bedroom and went to the closet. It was only a little ring. Two tiny white stones with a red one between them. She had seen it at Woolworth's last August when her mother had taken her and Annette shopping for school clothes. It was so pretty, and when she tried it on it fit perfectly. She didn't have the seventy-nine cents to buy it and knew it would be pointless to ask. She was just about to put the ring back when the saleslady turned to help another customer. Annette and her mother had moved on to the underwear section. Nicole slipped the ring into her pocket.

All the way home it had radiated heat. Though she would never be able to wear it — Annette and her mother would know where it had come from — it was hers now, and she could take it out and look at it whenever she wanted to. When she got home, she hid it in the hem of her winter coat.

She had looked at the ring a few times and then forgotten it. Now she would find it and take it back. Somehow, she would give it back.

Her fingers felt along the loosely stitched hem of the coat. Once. Twice. Nothing. She searched the floor of the closet, under and inside the shoes and boots, behind the stacked boxes of Snakes 'n' Ladders, Monopoly, and Checkers. Nothing. She pictured the ring falling from her coat and lying half-hidden in the dirt by the playground or in the dead weeds along the path to school. She imagined someone finding it, some girl who now wore it proudly. The ring that had made her a *thief*.

* * *

In January the hard cold came, settling among them like a stern relative. It froze the two small puddles in the corner of the yard. It frosted the windows and kept the oil stove in the living room rumbling all night. When Nicole and Annette walked back and forth to St. Agnes School, it bit at their cheeks and noses. Their booted feet chinked against the frozen earth like shovels.

There was only one thing to do on a Saturday afternoon, now that the cold had come. Now that the clothes on the line froze solid, now that the sheets and towels hung on the line like boards. With their skates tied together by the laces and looped over their shoulders, Nicole and Annette headed toward the pond. It was a quarter mile away, and as they walked, the cold made their teeth ache and their noses drip. The sky hung over them like a pale grey shawl.

Below Saint Patrick's Home For Boys, the square man-made pond was a picture of cheerfulness. Dozens of children and grownups glided across the ice. Their hellos and laughter rang against the cold like sounds at night. Someone had started a fire in one of the oil drums and a few people huddled around it, warming their hands.

Nicole and Annette found an empty bench, took off their boots, and put on their polished white skates. Soon they were on the ice, wobbling at first, then steadying. People they didn't know smiled at them, made room. A little silver cloud hovered around each face like a necklace.

On a low hill, a few hundred feet up from the pond, the huge old red brick Home loomed against the sky. Silent and gloomy, it contrasted sharply with the pond below, so full of happy, noisy, life. It occurred to Nicole that she had never seen any of the boys who lived there, though she walked by the Home everyday on her way back and forth to school. She imagined for a moment that the boys were all ugly and cruel-looking, with twisted faces and bad teeth, for surely that's what bad boys looked like. Then she remembered Billy. And she remembered the ring.

She wondered, suddenly, what it would be like to be locked up inside that cold, silent building, while sounds from the pond drifted up. Perhaps the boys were watching from their rooms, peering out from the sides of the windows so they couldn't be seen. Perhaps they were sorry for what they had done, and longed to be among the skaters, twirling freely and happily on the ice. She searched the uncurtained windows for faces.

"Look! I can still do an airplane," Annette said, spreading her arms and leaning forward. Nicole followed her, seeing how long she could hold up one leg without falling. The southeast corner of the pond seemed less crowded, so she skated over for a little more room to practice. Then she saw why there were so few skaters: the ice was grey-green, and a few feet beyond lay a patch of open water.

She paused at the edge of the safe area and stared at the water. Her father always warned them about thin ice, and every year there were stories of children falling through and drowning. How easy it would be, she thought, to go too far accidentally! She tried to imagine what it would be like, the moment you knew you could no longer turn back, the icy water licking at your ankles. She shuddered and skated back to the opposite side of the pond. Annette called her and they practiced their figure eights.

All afternoon Nicole caught herself searching the windows of the red brick building for faces. But all she saw was the empty glass, shimmering darkly like the patch of open water in the ice.

Ten

Evenings, after supper, her father immerses himself in the big armchair with the broken springs. Nicole watches him. His head tilts back, his jaw hangs loose. From the radio Carmen sings about love — *L'Amour, L'Amour* — her voice rising and falling in serrated passion. Nicole knows the music well; it is one of the four opera records her father plays over and over until her mother comes in and says all that shrieking is getting on her nerves.

The music catches Nicole in its hooks, that song in particular with its seductive ups and downs. With a sofa pillow for her partner, she prances and pirouettes through the room, stretching her neck like a swan. *I am Carmen. See how I was made to dance!* She eyes her father. *Do you see me? See how my body moves!* She tilts her head and lowers her eyes. *I am on stage. I am in the movies. Everyone who sees me is struck by my great beauty and sadness. Do you see me, Dad?*

André and Claude come in. "Oh look at that," they say, their mouths ugly with laughter. They grab the other pillows and flap at the air with their gangly arms and big feet. She is too noble to notice them, her dance too beautiful, too tragic. A pillow smacks against her head. She shrieks. Her father's face turns red. He hoists himself out of his chair: "Get out of here all of you! Can't I have a few moments' peace?"

* * *

I am ten. She draws the numbers on a patch of bare earth in the backyard, digging with the toe of her shoe. One, zero. Double digits. The world is opening like a clam. The world is sucking at her feet like the ocean.

* * *

Sunday noon. "No, I am not going to dry the dishes anymore. This is IT! I've had it. No more. The boys don't do anything. Annette will never let me wash. I'm not drying anymore." "Yes you are," from her mother. "NO. NO. NO. NO." "Charles, do something." "Do as your mother tells you!" "NO. NO. NO." Her father's face gets red like the inside of a watermelon. The veins at his temple bulge. His words come with a little shower of spit. "Yes you will!" He lunges heavily toward her. She is small and agile, and runs to the bathroom, her refuge. The lock is broken and part of the door jamb is missing from the many times she or Annette or André or Claude have crashed through in pursuit of someone fleeing, but she goes there anyway. It's the only place.

She anchors her feet against the edge of the cast iron bathtub and puts the full weight of her body against the door. *I am a flying buttress. I am a steel post. I am seventy-two pounds of levered strength.* Her father bangs on the door with his fists. "Come out of there right now!" She doesn't answer, saving her strength. He rams his body against the door. It moves a few inches, then slams shut again. She feels the blow in her legs, her arms, her lower back. "You WILL come out! You'll do as your mother tells you!" Again the door shudders violently. She pictures the red face, the flying spit. Her legs hold but she doesn't know for how much longer. "Come away Charles," she hears her mother say. "She'll come out eventually."

Nicole sits on the edge of the tub. How long will she have to stay in here? What will happen when she comes out? The house gets quiet. There's nothing for her to do. Someone comes toward the door. She wedges herself between the tub and the door again. "It's me," André says. "I have to do a number two." "Is it safe to come out now?" she asks. "Yes," he says. She tiptoes down the hall and peeps into the kitchen. No one is around. The dishes are stacked in the draining tray and spread out all over the counter. Drip-drying. She wipes the ones that are still wet and puts them all away.

* * *

I am ten. I could be Marilyn Monroe. She practices the throaty voice: *It's whanderful, it's mahvelous.* She combs her yellow hair over her eyes.

* * *

Annette is acting mysteriously. She won't let Nicole into the bathroom to wash her hands or look in the mirror while she's peeing. She always used to. She goes into their parents' bed room and closes the door. Peculiar. "What are you doing in there?" she asks. "Sneaking Mom's makeup?" Nicole sometimes does, and puts on her mother's earrings and necklaces and opens the vanity drawers to feel the balled up stockings and lace handkerchiefs and sweaters. "No, I'm not," Annette says. "I'm allowed in here. Mom knows I'm here." "What are you doing, then?" she asks again. Annette is leaning over the vanity, closing the bottom right drawer. "Nothing," she says, holding something behind her. "Nothing!"

What could it be, that thing wrapped in newspaper Annette won't show her? Is she sending secret messages to a boy? There are clues here. It must be boys. Why else would she look so suspicious? Thinking no one is looking, Annette slips the little packet into the waste basket by the basement stairs. When she leaves, Nicole hurries over, picks up the small bundle and slips down to the basement to unwrap it. Inside: a rectangular wad of cotton soaked with brownish-red blood. Oh.

* * *

I am ten. The moon is a big flat coin she wants to put in her pocket. The world pulls at her heart like the tide.

* * *

Her mother is going around talking in French again. Refusing to answer unless they at least *try* speaking in French. They are going to Digby County for the Acadian Festival. Two hundred years since the Deportation. There will be a Mass and a parade; some girl will get to be Evangeline, some boy, Gabriel.

Her mother is getting costumes ready. Flared skirts with white blouses and black bodices for her and Annette. And little white starched hats that look like nurses' caps. The boys will wear vests, too, and pull their socks up over the bottoms of their pants to make them look like knickers. They have big hats. André found a sea gull feather to put in his.

Tantes Yolande and Isabelle and Élise have been cooking all week. On Tante Yolande's kitchen table are huge pans of *pâté à la râpure* for the church supper after the parade. One is made with chicken, one with beef, the other with rabbit. "Sometimes they used veni-

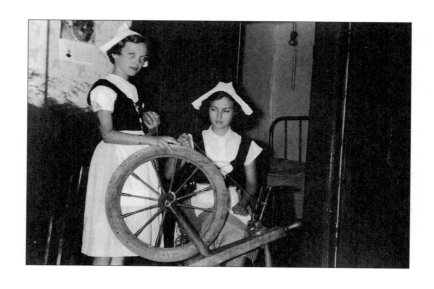

son, too," her mother says. "The Acadians had to survive on whatever was available, *ce qu'il y avait*. There were plenty of deer and rabbit in the woods, and potatoes and shallots to grow, and salt pork for flavor." Nicole looks at the brown crusts dotted with small cooked cubes of salt pork and feels her mouth water. Chicken *râpure* is her favourite.

Tante Yolande has made vests for her boys, too. Pierre, who has red cheeks and dark glinting eyes, walks around the kitchen in his. He wears tall black boots, and a small pouch hangs from his belt. Nicole looks at him shyly. He is the cutest boy she has ever seen, except that he is her cousin.

Soon they are all pulling things out of the closets and *le grenier* to put on the floats. An old spinning wheel, the butter churn from when Tante Isabelle and Nicole's mother were girls. Everyone is excited. Even frail old Grandmère, who sits in her rocker by the window, is smiling and eager. *"C'est une grande fête pour notre peuple,"* she says.

"It was horrible what the English did to the Acadians," her mother says. "We must never forget." Nicole has heard the story over and over, but today she pays more attention. They seem larger, more real, these ancestors, now that they are getting a parade to celebrate them.

"The soldiers separated families, sent people off on ships to anywhere that would take them," her mother continues. "Thousands died. Many never saw their loved ones again."

"How did we all get back?"

"Some who survived the Deportation came back, years later, when things had settled down. Others, who had gone into hiding in New Brunswick, Prince Edward Island, and parts of Cape Breton did too. When they arrived, after years of hardship, they found their lands confiscated, their homes burned. They had to start all over, here, along Saint Mary's Bay. Can you imagine what that must have been like?"

Her mother's face grows bitter with remembering, as if it had happened to her, personally, just a few years before.

"And Evangeline, did she ever come back?"

"No. She spent her whole life looking for Gabriel. She was young and beautiful, and he was the handsomest young man in the village. They were very much in love when they were separated, so she wanted desperately to find him. She followed his trail all over the United States, from New England to Louisiana to the Great Lakes. Though many young men begged her to marry them, she never would. She never gave up hope that she would find Gabriel. Finally, she became a Sister of Mercy, and one day, when she was nursing the sick in an almshouse, she recognized him. He died in her arms."

Each time her mother tells the story it is sadder, more beautiful; her mother's face softer, more wistful. Her mother has read them Longfellow's poem with its stirring first line — "This is the forest primeval" — but Nicole prefers the way her mother tells it. It's the most romantic story Nicole has ever heard. Even more romantic than *Carmen*. It's a story of True Love. And some girl would get to be Evangeline. Some boy, Gabriel.

"Her real name was Emmeline La Biche," her mother says. "She's buried in Louisiana."

* * *

I am ten. Oh, the sadness of love! The apple tree in the yard and the wedge of blue ocean at the horizon pierce her with their beauty.

* * *

So many people have come! Already they line the highway where the parade will pass. Oncle Louie harnesses the two big work horses to the hay wagon decorated with several Acadian flags — the tricolor with the star of Mary — and a sign that reads: *L'Acadie 1755-1955*. Old Monsieur Boudreau brings out his two black oxen, and twists wild roses around their horns. And all the priests are there, even the Monseigneur in his scarlet vestments. During Mass, he stands on a raised platform and moves his eyes over the crowd. "We must never forget our church, our language, and our history," he says. "They are what make us *Les Acadiens*. We have suffered as a people, but we have triumphed over our suffering."

Everyone who owns a car has it clean and decorated, ready for the parade. And the floats — some show the church in Grande Pré where the Acadians were rounded up; others with dikes show the lands along

Minas Basin that the Acadians had reclaimed from the sea before the English seized them. Several men and boys, dressed like British soldiers, pretend to guard a group of Acadians. Their expressions are rough and hateful. The Acadians look brave and sad.

What is her mother saying? *She* is to be Evangeline! And Pierre is to be Gabriel! They are to sit here, on this float, under these *pâpier maché* trees that represent the Forest Primeval — *l'Acadie* in its happiest days. Can this really be happening?

The parade is starting. Everyone is singing, *Ave, Maris Stella, Dei Mater alma* . . . the national anthem of the Acadians. Hundreds of Acadians line the highway, all looking at her and Pierre as they pass, their mouths open in song. Her mother, her father, even her brothers are singing. Many of the old people are crying.

She looks at Pierre beside her, standing so straight and tall. His hand is almost touching hers. She sees herself following him through the woods, her heart sick with longing, knowing that he, too, searches for her. Other boys would ask for her hand but she would turn away, faithful and true. She finds him on a hospital bed, dying. She holds him in her arms and they kiss goodbye. Music swells.

* * *

I am ten. She tilts her head to one side, her face tragic. *I am an Acadian.* The world shimmers with sadness and beauty.

She Wouldn't Want Them

"I love you so much," Lynne says, her pale face shining.

"Oh darling," I say, lifting my face to meet hers.

We kiss, our lips clenched shut. We are sprawled on the bed in Lynne's bedroom, on her white chenille bedspread. It's the kind of bedroom I have always wanted, with its pink and white flowered wallpaper, a soft rug instead of linoleum. The late afternoon sun filters through the frilly white curtains, making everything look soft and golden.

"It's your turn to be the man now," Lynne says. Her heart-shaped face bobs forward and her brown curls jiggle. "What's your name going to be?"

"I'll be Al." Al is my favourite name for a man.

"I'll be Rosemary," Lynne says. "Isn't that the most beautiful name? Rose-mary. Like roses."

We take our positions on the edge of the bed.

"Oh, Rosemary," I begin. "You're so beautiful!"

"And you're so handsome, Al!"

"I love you so much, Rosemary!" I put my arms around her. "Will you marry me?"

"Oh, Al!" Our dry lips meet and we collapse on the bed in a passionate embrace.

This is Lynne's favourite game. I'm not as enthusiastic about it as Lynne is, but at eleven, I figure it'll be good practice for when a real boy wants to kiss me.

"You hurt my neck that time," Lynne said, sitting up.

The voice of Lynne's grandfather drifts up from the yard. "Are you girls still up there?"

We go over to the window. "Yes we are," Lynne calls down. Her grandfather, a small wiry man with a slight limp, looks up at us from his roses. There are rows and rows of them, in every color imaginable: pink, yellow, red, white, peach. He's always tying them up, pruning them, spraying them, or pulling out weeds with his small, gnarled hands.

"It's time for your friend to go home now," he says.

Lynne's grandfather takes care of Lynne after school. Her mother is seldom home, though I have no idea where she is all the time.

"Why don't you come to *my* house tomorrow after school," I suggest.

"I don't know," she says. "It's so far."

My house is on the other side of the school, in a different neighborhood. "I could show you all the candy in our basement," I coax. Lynne has never been to my house; I've been going to her house since last year in grade five.

When I get home I find my mother in the kitchen peeling potatoes for supper. Dirty dishes cover the counters and sink; the pot we used at noon to warm up the beans in sits on the stove, all dried and crusty.

"Nicole," my mother says, "it would be nice if on the days I substitute teach you and Annette would come home after school and clean up a bit."

"Sorry," I say, "I forgot."

"I can't do everything. If I have to help your father earn a living you kids have to pitch in and help, too."

"I know, Mom. I just forgot today."

"You could at least clear the table and put the dirty dishes in the sink at noon. When I'm not here, it seems you all do whatever you feel like doing."

At noon, we'd found the back door unlocked, which meant that my father wouldn't be home. Without him, we couldn't agree on what to eat. Annette and Claude and I ate the beans with bread and butter, but André opened a can of Campbell's soup. Afterward, we opened a large can of peaches and ate them all. The empty can stares at me from its puddle of syrup. I feel a sudden urge to take all the dirty dishes and pots and pans and throw them in the garbage.

"Are you substituting tomorrow?" I ask.

"No. Three days in one week is enough." Her shoulders droop. "But you never know, they might call."

When they call, usually at 7:00 A.M., my mother tears through the house getting herself ready. The rest of us have to wait in line for the bathroom. My mother puts on a nice dress and powder and lipstick, but by the time we all leave, the house is a wreck. I wouldn't want Lynne to come over on one of those days.

The phone doesn't ring the following morning, so my mother makes pancakes. Before I leave for school I make the bed, even though it's Annette's turn, and take some of the junk off our dresser. Maybe Lynne would come over.

At recess, Lynne and Judy and I meet by the school canteen where they sell moon pies, chocolate bars, and bags of peanuts and chips. My father supplies the chips. I have a bag of honeymoons from home, so I'm not buying anything. The chocolate coating discolored so my father can't sell them.

"Are you coming over to my house today?" I ask Lynne.

"I can't," Lynne says. "I have to go somewhere with my grandpa."

Judy buys a Crispy Crunch and gives me a piece. I give her three honeymoons in return.

"Are these from your father's basement?" she asks.

"Yes. You should come over and see it. Why don't you come today, since Lynne can't?"

"I wish I could, but you know my father won't let me. He hardly ever lets me go anywhere." Judy shakes her head and two thick black waves of hair swing forward into pretty little points along her cheeks. My own hair is thin and yellow, and no matter what I do to it, the front sticks out like cat's whiskers. "You could come to my house, though," she says.

The houses in Judy's neighborhood are larger than those in mine and are made of brick instead of wood and asbestos shingles. I've been to Judy's house only twice before, and as we walk under the high elms, along tidy green lawns bordered with asters and chrysanthemums, I try to imagine what it would be like to live there. Everything is neat and pretty, but unlike my neighborhood, there are hardly any children playing in the yards.

When we get to the house, we head for the kitchen to see Mrs. Ryan, the housekeeper. Judy's mother died of TB when Judy was four.

"How are you hon," Mrs. Ryan says to Judy. Mrs. Ryan is short and stout and has a dark complexion. "I see you brought your little friend again."

She puts out a plate of cookies and pours two glasses of milk. I think how nice it would be to have my mother waiting for me with a glass of milk and a plate of cookies when I come home from school. But since my mother started substitute teaching, she hardly ever makes cookies anymore. When she does, they seldom last more than a day. My mother is much prettier than Mrs. Ryan though, I note, eyeing Mrs. Ryan's thick, muscular arms.

Upstairs, we sit on Judy's bed and look at pictures of her brother, who is nineteen and away at college in New Brunswick. His room, across the hall, is neat and silent, just like Judy's.

"He comes home about once a month," Judy says.

I think how lovely it would be to have an older brother, instead of two bratty, younger brothers who mess up everything and torment me all the time. But Judy doesn't have a basement full of candy, I reflect.

"I wish your father would let you come to my house some time."

"Me too," Judy says. "Oh, I almost forgot. He said I could go downtown tomorrow after school, as long as I'm with someone."

It will be our second such excursion. On Fridays the downtown stores stay open until 6:00. That means we'll have two whole hours to wander through Zellers and Woolworths trying on rhinestone rings and fondling nylon scarves; two whole hours to stare at the women's underwear, to poke our fingers through the cages at the budgies.

"Great," I say. "Lynne's coming too."

Just as I am about to leave, Judy's father comes home. I have never seen him before, and with his grey suit, white shirt and striped tie, he looks as though he has just come from church instead of work. He's much younger than my own father and has dimples like Judy's. He puts his hat and briefcase on the sofa and says, "Hello girls."

"This is Nicole," Judy says. He smiles and shakes my hand. I feel, suddenly, as though I am wearing my best dress.

The next morning at recess I see a familiar figure shuffling down the hall ahead of me. I recognize my father's old jacket and baggy pants, his grey cap, the yellow pencil hooked over his left ear. I have never actually seen him make his deliveries at the school before, and my first impulse is to call out. Then I check myself. The halls are full of kids. What would they think if they saw him? A picture of Judy's father in his suit and tie flashes before me. I duck into the lavatory, my ears and cheeks burning.

When I come out, my father is safely gone. After the initial relief, a wave of remorse seizes me. Why did I do such a thing? A group of girls from grade three and four are standing by the canteen eating potato chips. "My father's a candyman," I hiss as I pass. "He's the one who brought those chips you're eating."

After school, Judy and Lynne and I hurry over to the trolley stop, a few blocks away.

"Are you going to buy anything today?" Judy asks.

"I don't know," I say. "Are you?"

"I might buy a nylon scarf," Lynne says.

When the trolley arrives, humming like a giant insect, its antennae fastened to a web of suspended wire, we drop our dimes into the chute and head for the back seat. From there we can see everything: the fat lady jiggling her body down the aisle, the man with a curled mustache, the girl with thick glasses and tiny eyes. The trolley twists around the corner and makes a sudden screeching sound. A shower of sparks falls outside the window behind us, the bus stops, and the driver hurries around to the back. He pulls down the two long cords that attach the trolley poles to the electric wires and quickly releases them. Instead of hooking back on, the poles miss and the wires spit and hiss. "Damn!" the driver shouts. "God Damn!" It takes two more tries

along with two more "God-damns" and one "son-of-a-bitch," words we are forbidden to hear, before the bus starts up again. We put our hands over our mouths and roll our eyes. The back seat is definitely the best place.

It's a twenty minute ride downtown, and as the bus jerks and lurches from corner to corner, I begin to feel queasy. I stick my head out the window and gulp a few breaths of air.

"What's the matter with you," Lynne asks. "You look funny."

"I feel a little sick," I reply. "I'll be okay when we get there." Lynne and Judy exchange glances. But the wind in my face doesn't help. My head feels hot, my blouse sticky, and my stomach . . .

"We're here!" Judy calls out, finally. I hold my hands over my mouth and bolt off the bus. Too late. Leaning against a wall to keep from falling, I begin vomiting, horribly, profusely, right in front of Zellers. I am vaguely aware of people passing, staring, of the spectacle I am creating. But the world is spinning, and I can't help myself.

Finally, it's over. I look around for Judy and Lynne but they are nowhere in sight. I realize, suddenly, that I'm all alone. I don't even have a handkerchief to wipe my mouth with, and my legs are trembling. I begin to cry.

A woman steps out of the crowd and hands me a wad of Kleenex. "Where do you live, little girl?"

I give her my address and the woman steers me gently to a car waiting by the curb. I am much too miserable to remember my mother's warnings about strangers and their cars, so I follow willingly. Once in the car, I begin feeling better.

"What happened to you?" the woman asks. "How come you were all by yourself?"

I tell her about the bus ride, about Judy and Lynne.

"Maybe they went to get help," the woman says. "One of them should have stayed with you, though."

By now I am feeling well enough to contemplate their treacherous behavior, to consider what I might say to them Monday at school. But I am also well enough to notice the woman's lipstick, an orangy-pink, the same color as her scarf. And the car we are riding in: brand new and smelling of leather. I look at the woman's powdered face, at her hair, the color of MacIntosh toffee, and think of the woman in the billboards advertizing Moirs chocolates. Dressed in a black velvet gown, she accepts the black and gold box from a handsome man. Rosemary, I think. Her name has to be Rosemary.

Suddenly I feel lucky to be riding in her car, lucky that this woman found me — *rescued* me, really — from that awful humiliation. I stare at her in admiration and damp gratitude. She looks over at me and smiles.

"I'm glad to see you're feeling better." Her hands on the steering wheel are white and smooth, her fingernails long and pink. She begins asking me questions about myself, my family, what my father does for a living.

"My father's a candyman," I tell her. "We have a whole basement full of candy. You should see it, boxes and boxes of chocolate buds, spearmint leaves, red and black licorice, jaw breakers, marshmallow bananas, honeymoons, coconut balls . . . " I pause to catch my breath. "There are lots more, but I can't remember them all."

The woman smiles again, so I continue. "We also have Bub's bubble gum and potato chips. My father sells them to grocery stores. The best part is that when a box of candy gets broken or crushed, we get to eat it." I don't tell her that sometimes the discolored chocolate tastes funny, or that the squashed or melted candy is sometimes so unappealing that even my brother Claude won't eat it.

"How nice for you," the woman says. Her eyes are green, a yellowy green like new leaves in spring.

"My father will probably give you a nice big box of candy as a reward for bringing me home," I tell her.

"That won't be necessary," the woman says, but a little smile plays around the edges of her mouth, so I know she is pleased. What a lovely woman she is! So pretty and nice. I picture my mother inviting her in for tea and taking out our good china cups. Two pretty women, my mother with her dark hair and red lipstick, Rosemary with her toffee-colored hair and orangy-pink lipstick, sipping tea together, talking and smiling. They would become best friends; then my mother and I would go over to her house to visit, like I go to Judy's and Lynne's.

When we arrive, my mother meets us at the door. She has on an old apron and house dress, and she isn't wearing lipstick.

"I found her throwing up in front of Zellers," the woman explains. "Her friends had left her. She seems to be all right now, though."

My mother's eyes search me in astonishment. "Thank you so much!" she says. "You were very kind to help her."

The woman turns and begins going down the steps. It isn't supposed to go like this, I think. It's all happening too fast. "Mom, quick, offer her a box of candy," I whisper.

"Don't be silly," my mother says. "She wouldn't want one."

Mortified, I watch the woman's car pull away. I had virtually promised her a box of candy. What would she think of me now? Yet, as I picture my mother handing the woman a box of spearmint leaves or honeymoons, I realize with sudden clarity that my mother is right. She wouldn't want them. I realize too, with a little shock of pain, that I will never see the woman again.

Will Someone Tell Me, Please?

1
Evening Eye

Annette and her friend Babbette lie on our bed whispering, and when I come in they stop.

"What are you talking about?"

"Nothing," they say.

"Tell me."

"Nothing, really." They look at each other, then look away. Annette picks a bit of fluff off the bedspread.

"Then you won't mind if I sit here and read." I plop myself down at the desk. Annette's leg starts thumping up and down on the pink comforter.

"Why don't you go downstairs and read," she says. "I don't butt in when you have Colleen over."

True. But all Colleen and I ever do is play rummy. And Babbette knows things. She's always whispering things to Annette that make her giggle. I want to know too.

Babbette has light brown hair, shoulder-length, and naturally curly. She wears it parted on one side and falling over her face like Rita Hayworth. Her nose is a bit too big and her front teeth stick out, but you'd think she was a movie star, the way she walks.

Annette sits in the desk chair, her face tilted up as though she's praying. Babbette bends over her. "This is how you make your eyes look wider," Babbette says, plucking the tiny hairs on the bridge of Annette's nose. "Never pluck above the eyebrow itself, though." They rub white grease all over their faces, making circles around their eyes so they look like big owls.

"You should cream your face every day," Babbette says in her expert's voice, "to keep your skin soft and silky." My mother creams her face every night at the big round vanity mirror, but I never knew it was important until Babbette said it was. "It wouldn't do *you* any good though," Babbette tells me, giving me one of her closed-lip smiles. "You're too young." When Babbette smiles like that she reminds me of a bulldog. I smile back sweetly.

Annette and Babbette are both fourteen and have breasts. Seeing Annette in her pointy bra and half slip makes me ill. I've never seen Babbette without her clothes on but she's tall and looks terrific in a sweater.

At twelve and a half I'm still flat as a boy. Sometimes I stand in front of the mirror and think about all the things I don't have and all the things I don't know. When no one is looking I shift my white camisole around until my pink nipples poke through the little eyelet holes. Annette has had breasts since she was eleven.

Annette is standing in front of the mirror in her bra and panties. I can see a shadow where the hair is. I'm sprawled on the bed with my new magazine, *Hit Songs of 1957*.

"Where are you going?" I ask.

"Nowhere," she says, pulling her dark hair into a neat pony tail high on the back of her head.

"You must be going someplace or you wouldn't be fixing yourself up."

"Babbette's coming over and we're going for a walk, that's all." She leans into the mirror and dabs her eyelashes with a small square brush.

"Can I come?"

"No."

"Why not?"

"You have your own friends, Nicole; why don't you go for a walk with Colleen?" She's putting on pink lipstick now, making little sucking noises, almost kissing herself in the mirror.

"I know where you're going," I say in my most casual voice. Annette turns with her hands on her hips, her high breasts pointing straight at me.

"Where, smartypants?"

"You're going down to the playground at the army barracks." That stops her. Little sparks fly out of her eyes. I didn't know for sure they were going there. Now I do.

"Maybe we are and maybe we aren't." She clicks the words coldly. "It's none of your business."

I watch her pull a sleeveless white blouse off its hanger and put it on. "Maybe it is and maybe it isn't," I say. "You know Dad doesn't like you to go there."

She whirls around at this, her nostrils twitching, her face pink. "That's too bad, and you'd better not tell him if you know what's good for you!"

"What will you do, beat me up?" I flutter my eyelashes.

She yells, "I can't wait till the end of the summer when I'll have my own room and finally be rid of you!"

Mr. McNair has been hammering and sawing the area across the hall into a new room for Annette. I'll have this room to myself pretty soon, but I'm not sure how I feel about that.

When Babbette arrives, her bra straps showing through the wide arms of her sleeveless blouse, Annette whispers something to her and they go off arm in arm. I watch them from the bedroom window for a moment, then rush downstairs and telephone Colleen.

"Come over right away," I tell her. I can hear one of the babies crying in the background. "Run if you have to."

In less than two minutes Colleen appears, wearing her old dungarees, panting and smelling like a kitchen full of dirty dishes. Colleen doesn't have breasts either.

"It's Annette and Babbette," I tell her. "They're up to something." Colleen grins and her pale eyes scrunch up.

When we reach the barracks, the sun is just touching the roofs of the houses on the other side of the street, and the cinder block buildings in the compound glow faintly pink. We crouch behind some bushes a few yards from the playground, near the wire mesh fence that surrounds the barracks. Children's voices rise and fall in play.

"Can you see them?" Colleen asks, craning her thin neck forward.

"Right over there, on the second set of swings."

Annette and Babbette are swinging themselves slowly, letting their feet scuff the hollows of dirt carved into the grass. A few older boys hang around by the poles, talking and looking over at them. Small rings of laughter rise and encircle them, but we can't hear what any of them are saying. Suddenly a boy with a dark crewcut and black T-shirt lets out a howl and shimmies up the pole by the swing. He crawls across the top pole then drops, dangling by his legs upside down above Annette and Babbette. They shriek and leap off the swings, then run to the side poles, holding their hands over their mouths and giggling.

The other boys cheer. The dark boy pulls himself back up, shimmies down the pole and lands at their feet, grinning. His teeth flash white. Annette and Babbette begin talking to the cluster of boys now. Small chunks of words drift over. He went *there*. Oh *sure*.

Really. The words blink off and on, infuriatingly, like fireflies.

"What are they saying?" Colleen asks. "I can't hear them."

Babbette keeps throwing her head back, flinging the wave of curly brown hair backward, then leaning forward the next minute and letting it fall over her face again. Annette moves her hands up and down the poles, as if she isn't sure where to put them. The boys scuff their feet and snort like ponies.

"What are they doing? Can you see?"

"This is boring," I say after a while. My legs have started to cramp from crouching so long. "We'd better get home before it gets completely dark."

"I don't see what the big deal is anyway," Colleen mutters as we walk.

I don't either, but I don't say anything. I am remembering the last time: my father's face, red and bloated; Annette's, white and stiff. *Those boys are wild! They'll get you in trouble!* my father shouted. *In trouble*, he kept saying, spitting out the words like dark, ugly seeds. I tried to imagine what he meant, picturing Annette and Babbette breaking windows or starting fires with a small band of barrack boys. Somehow that didn't seem right. What could he mean? They weren't doing *anything*.

I stare at the evening star for a while, hanging in the western sky like an eye. The evening eye.

Maybe he meant smoking.

2
Strawberry Jam

It's never been this quiet before. Even Ronnie, who has to sit at the back of the class because he's such a troublemaker, isn't making a peep. The only sound is Mrs. Casey's voice, rasping and gurgling through the room like something metallic and rusted. My mother says it's from a lifetime of smoking, and that's how Annette and I will sound if we ever start.

We all like Mrs. Casey because she tells us things — what it's like to be in a coal mining disaster like her brother was in Sydney; what makes the earth red in Prince Edward Island; or what her sister has to put up with, living in Newfoundland with her fisherman husband and eight children.

Today she's telling us about our bodies.

"When your bodies start to change, to become adult, your odors change," she says. Kevin's face turns pink and he stares at his knuckles. Doreen's eyes fasten on Kathy's back. Colleen, in the front row, slumps over.

"It's perfectly normal," Mrs. Casey continues, "Only some people find those adult odors offensive."

I try to figure out who she could mean. She isn't looking at anyone in particular, though it's hard to tell because her glasses are so thick. Nancy, sitting in front of me, shifts a little. Nancy has curly black hair and a pink mouth shaped like a rosebud. She also has breasts, though she's not stuck-up about them like some of the other girls. Could Mrs. Casey mean Nancy? I edge my nose closer to Nancy's back, to her red sweater indented at the shoulders where the bra straps dig in. She smells of shampoo and warm wool. And something else. I don't know what it is, exactly, but it's a pleasant smell, a little like my mother smells in the morning.

"There are many kinds of deodorant available at the pharmacy," Mrs. Casey's voice rumbles on. "But even more important, some of you need to bathe more frequently."

Who could she mean? Cathy Dunford used to come to school smelling of pee. Everyone said there were only two beds in their house and that the big kids had to sleep with the little kids who wet the bed all the time. But that was a while ago, and Cathy's in another class now.

Maybe she means Carolyn. She's almost fifteen and should be in grade nine but she was held back twice. She wears lipstick and teases up the front of her red hair so it sticks out and makes her look like a rooster. The more I think about it, the more I'm sure Mrs. Casey means Carolyn. And probably her friend, Diane. They both wear pointy bras and tight sweaters. They must be the ones with the adult odors. I try to glance at them out of the corner of my eye, to see if they know Mrs. Casey is talking about them, but they sit a few rows behind me so I can't without being obvious.

After class, everyone files out silently. Colleen, waiting for me down the hall, rolls her eyes and whispers, "Would you tell me if it were me?"

"Of course," I say, wondering if I really would. Colleen always smells a bit like unrinsed milk bottles, but I don't think that's what Mrs. Casey means.

"Well?" she whispers again.

"Well, what?"

"Do I?" She looks worried.

"No, you don't." I wonder if she half wishes she did, because maybe that would mean she'd finally get breasts. Or maybe that's just what I'm wishing.

Near the corner we find ourselves walking behind Carolyn and Diane and a few other girls. Carolyn is a foot taller than Diane and they both look angry all the time. Even when they're laughing they look like they're mad at something.

"I think Mrs. Casey means them," I whisper. Colleen stares at Carolyn and Diane. Colleen and I often tell each other how stupid Carolyn and Diane look with their weird hairdos and bright lipstick, the way they walk as if nothing ever bothers them. Neither of them has ever spoken to us. I often wonder what they talk about with their friends, what they do on weekends. Somehow I can't picture them playing rummy or Monopoly like Colleen and I do. Someone said they get into fights with other girls and let boys kiss them. I don't know about the fights, but I wouldn't mind having a boy kiss me. I wish I knew how they get them to do it.

Carolyn is wearing a white sweater set and a green felt skirt with a poodle on the front. I stare at her skirt swishing above her bobby socks and saddle shoes, thinking how nice it would be to have one just like it.

Then I notice a spot on the back. She must have sat in something, I conclude, something sticky and red. Suddenly I think: I could tell her. A small thrill passes through me, picturing Carolyn smiling gratefully at me.

"Carolyn!" I call out. Colleen's eyes pop open.

Carolyn turns and glares down at me. "What?" she says. The other girls stop, turn, and stare at me.

I swallow and say, "You have a red spot on the back of your skirt. You must have sat in some strawberry jam."

Carolyn pulls her skirt around and looks at it. She mumbles something to Diane and they bend over to inspect the skirt. The other girls look, too. "Strawberry jam," Carolyn says looking at me with a peculiar expression. Then she breaks into wild laughter. In a flash, all the other girls are laughing, too. Carolyn takes off her cardigan and ties it around her waist so it hangs over the spot. Then they all cross the street shrieking with laughter. Someone yells out "Strawberry jam!" and they all laugh again, even louder.

"What's the matter with them?" I ask Colleen. "I just thought she should know."

Colleen scuffs her feet and stares at the sidewalk. "I don't think it was strawberry jam," she says in a low voice. Suddenly, I get it. I realize, too, that I'll never be able to show my face in public again. I might as well leave right now and become a missionary in Africa.

3
How

"But *how* does it get there?" I ask my mother, determined to get an answer this time. She's holding the other end of the sheet we're folding, rubbing the frozen edges to soften them. Annette is ironing dry a damp pillow case, her back to us, her shoulders tense with listening. Steam curls against the window; the kitchen smells like the wind outside.

"Did you read the booklet I gave you?" my mother asks, not looking at me.

"I read it three times, and Annette did too, didn't you Annette." Annette turns and nods. "But it doesn't tell *how* it happens, just that it *does*."

My mother puts the folded sheet on the table with the others. I study her face for clues. "It just happens," she says, reaching for another sheet.

André comes in then and heads for the bread drawer. We finished the supper dishes less than an hour ago now there he is, cutting two big slabs of bread and coating them with margarine and molasses, dirtying a plate, two knives, and leaving bread crumbs all over the counter. My mother and I fold three more sheets. None of us says anything until André takes his plate out to the living room where he and Claude and my father are watching *The Honeymooners*.

"What do you mean it just happens? Do the man and the woman have to *do* anything?" Annette stops ironing and listens.

"When a man and a woman get married," my mother begins, "They sleep in the same bed. Then it happens."

I'm waiting to hear the rest but she turns and starts folding undershirts. "*What* happens?" I push. "Is it automatic?" I know that the sperm come out of some part of the man and somehow get into the woman, but I don't know how. I imagine them as small, blind worms, hunting frantically until they find the egg.

"It's natural," my mother says twisting her face as though the words hurt her mouth.

They must just crawl across the sheet, I'm thinking. If I flung the blankets off some sleeping couple I would see dozens of tiny white worms groping their way toward the woman.

"If I slept in the same bed as a man, would it happen?" I picture the men I know, Mr. Smith next door, Mr. Penny across the street, my mother's cousin Percy. I wouldn't want to be in the same bed with any of them, but I need to know. It doesn't occur to me that this could apply to boys, too.

My mother looks at me sharply. "You haven't started your period yet. Are you sure you read the booklet?"

I'd forgotten that part. "Well what about Annette? Would she have a baby if she slept in the same bed as a man?"

My mother bites the edge of her lip. "Men and women don't sleep in the same bed unless they're married. It happens after you're married."

Maybe there are no little worms, I'm thinking now. Maybe it's more mysterious, like in mass with the bread and wine. It must be like that. When a man and woman say the wedding vows, the man's sperm automatically enters the woman's body, just like Christ's body enters the host when the priest says the words. They don't have to do anything. It all happens invisibly.

"That's not right," Annette says later when I tell her my theory. "I know the man and woman have to do something."

We're lying across my bed looking at drawings of a tiny baby curled inside its mother's womb. My room is warmer than Annette's but we're both wrapped in quilts. "*What?*" I ask.

"I'm not sure," she says.

"How about Babbette? Does she know?"

Annette shrugs and traces the outline of the mother's stomach with her finger. I wonder if she knows more than she's letting on. Something in her look makes me remember things I've heard kids say. Things I always thought they'd made up.

"If you were married and wanted a baby," I begin cautiously, "and you had to do something disgusting to get one, would you do it?"

"I don't know," she says, looking away. "Maybe."

I lie there in my quilt contemplating this, and for a brief moment the dark mystery opens up with all its terrible truth. No, I think. It couldn't be that. Could it? The wind rattles against the storm windows, making them sound like chattering teeth.

Nothing Ever Happens

"You move your hand in a circular motion," Babbette says, making small, quick circles over her leg. "And you do only a small area at a time."

"What's all that white powder?" Annette asks.

"That's from the mitt. It makes your legs feel silky." She holds out her leg. "Feel."

Annette and I touch her leg. It feels like velvet.

"When the hair grows back it doesn't leave a stubble like shaving does," Babbette explains.

Annette takes the other mitt and begins rubbing her right leg, making circles in time to the Jimmy Rodgers song playing on the small, boxy record player: I *as*-ked her to *mar*-ry and *be* my sweet *wi*-fe . . .

"Having beautiful legs is really important," Babbette says. "I read an article about it in *Chatelaine*. If your calves are in the right place you'll have beautiful legs."

"How can you tell if your calves are in the right place?" I ask.

"Easy," Babbette says. "When you put your feet together like this, the inside of your calves should almost touch. See?"

Annette and I jump up and put our feet together. My calves are about an inch apart, but the space between Annette's is as wide as a hairbrush. Annette gasps and stares at her legs as though they were covered with warts.

"It'll take a lot of work," Babbette sighs, "but you might be able to fix that."

"How?"

"There are leg exercises. First you put your toes together and spread your heels."

Annette and I put our toes together and spread our heels.

"Now concentrate on the calf muscles and try to move them inward without moving your heels." We watch Babbette's calf muscles twitch and do the same with our own.

"You have to do this at least ten minutes a day for it to do any good," Babbette warns. We twitch our calf muscles to the music: She *ha*-ad *ki*-sses *swee*-ter than *wi*-ne . . .

"What are you wearing tonight?" Annette asks Babbette.

"My new blue with the white flowers. How about you?"

"My red," Annette says. Annette's red dress hugs all the curves of her body and the little cup sleeves teeter provocatively on her shoulders. Though she's only sixteen, Annette looks at least eighteen when she wears that dress. I tried it on once, but it was baggy at the breasts and too tight around the waist. I'm fourteen.

"Didn't you wear your red dress to the K.C. dance last weekend?" I ask. Annette stops twitching and stiffens.

"So what?"

"I bet you're really going to the Jubilee." I say, making my voice low and confidential, so they'll know I can be trusted. Annette is forbidden to go to the Jubilee, but she and Babbette go anyway. Sailors hang out there, and you're supposed to be eighteen.

Annette and Babbette exchange glances. Then Annette looks at me narrowly. "If I tell you," she says, "promise you won't tell Mom?"

After supper, Colleen comes over and we sit on the front steps.

"You want to finish the Monopoly game we started the other day?" she asks.

"I don't know," I say. I'm feeling restless and angry at the same time, but I don't know why.

"You want to play Red Rover, then?" A bunch of kids are playing a rowdy game of it on the street.

I give her an icy look. "You must be kidding. We're starting high school in a few weeks, remember?"

"Well it's something to do. Besides, you thought it was fun last time."

A big black ant appears on the bottom step. I squash it with my sneaker. Another appears. I squash it too. I keep thinking how Babbette and Annette looked when they left, whispering things to each other, their eyes flashing, as if something important were about to happen.

"Nothing ever happens around here," I say.

Colleen shrugs. "What do you want to have happen?"

"I don't know — *anything!*"

We watch the Red Rover game for a few minutes. Each team has five or six kids and they're all shrieking and crashing into each other. Mrs. Kolb and Mrs. MacKenzie go clickety-click up the street on their high heels. Every two Saturdays they play Bingo while their husbands babysit.

"Annette and Babbette went to the Jubilee tonight," I tell Colleen.

"They did?"

"And I'll bet you anything that Annette's meeting Emile there."

"You mean that guy she's not supposed to go out with? That older guy?"

"Annette says he's twenty-one, but my mother says he's even older than that. Annette meets him places. You should have heard the big row she and my mother had about him last week."

"Oh wow!" Colleen says.

"I know how we can find out."

"How?"

"He lives a few blocks past Johnny's, on Young Street. We could walk by and see if his truck's there."

Colleen's eyes get big. "Let's!"

The streets are thronged with people — kids playing jump rope and hide-and-seek, teenagers walking around in small groups eyeing each other, couples wheeling baby carriages. Whole families sit on their front porches like spectators waiting for a parade. No one wants to be inside during the last warm evenings of summer. Any day now the change will come as it always does in mid-August. The evenings will turn cool; summer will be over.

"Let's get an ice cream," I suggest. Johnny's is just up ahead. "Do you have any money?"

"A dime."

"Good, so do I."

We sit at the stainless steel counter and watch a pair of boys work the pinball machine in the corner. One of them lives down the street from me. A box of Export A's and a book of matches bulge from the rolled-up sleeve of his white T-shirt, and as he jerks the controls, the muscles in his upper arms ripple. After he finishes the game, he looks around to see who else is in the store. He doesn't seem to notice Colleen and me.

"What will you have?" Johnny asks us. He's a short, dark man with big hands that wave around as he talks. Colleen orders a chocolate cone.

"I'll have grapenut." Grapenut sounds like a flavor an older girl might order. Colleen looks at me and makes a face.

When we come out, we see Carolyn and Diane talking to a few boys in front of the store. Carolyn is wearing the oddest pair of pedal pushers I have ever

seen: The front of one leg is black, and the back, white; the front of the other leg is white, and the back, black.

"Will you look at that," I mutter under my breath. "Too bad she doesn't have white paint on her face, too."

"And a big red wig," Colleen adds, sputtering into her cone. "She'd look exactly like a clown."

"She already has a big red wig," I say, referring to Carolyn's red hair.

"We'd better not laugh too hard," Colleen says. "What if she's in my class at St. Pat's this year?"

"She might be. For sure she won't be in mine."

Suddenly things aren't funny any more. Colleen and I both get quiet and I know we are thinking about the same thing.

"You know I didn't want to take those scholarship exams," I tell her. "My mother made me."

"I know."

"Nothing will change though, really."

Colleen doesn't say anything and we walk along quietly, eating our cones. Everyone I know will be going to St. Pat's.

That's where Annette and her friends all go. But I'll be going to the Sacred Heart Convent School — with all the rich girls from the South End, and no boys. *You'll have a chance to make something of yourself,* my mother's been saying all summer. They put my picture in the paper when I won, and the teachers at Saint Catherine's told me they were proud of me. But the kids, except for Colleen, began giving me strange looks, as if I were someone they didn't know.

When we round the corner on to Young Street, the street lights blink on. Streaks of pink and orange feather the sky. "Which house is it?" Colleen asks, licking the last of the ice cream from her fingers.

"Don't worry, we'll find it. You know the funniest part of all this is that Emile and my father do the same thing."

"You mean Emile is a candyman?"

"Sort of. He and his brothers sell chocolate bars and bags of candy, though they don't sell penny candy. They sell other stuff, too, like nylons and cigarette lighters. They call them 'novelties'."

"How come you know so much about it?" Colleen looks at me suspiciously.

"My father knows him."

When Emile first came to our house earlier in the summer, my father was arranging boxes in the back of the truck; I was sitting on the front steps waiting to see what Annette's new boyfriend looked like. A truck like my father's pulled up in front of our house and a tall, slim man stepped out, dressed in a dark suit and tie. Something about his big square jaw, his dark oiled hair piled over his forehead, made him look important. My father said, "Well," and shook his hand. He kept smiling at the man with a peculiar smile and shifting from foot to foot. I couldn't figure it out. My father wasn't expecting anyone, but I didn't think a grown up man would be coming for Annette. In a few moments Annette came bouncing down the steps, her pony tail and breasts bobbing, the sleeves of her red dress half falling off her shoulders. My mother stood at the door watching. She smiled and waved, but the corners of her mouth were twitching.

After they left, my mother snapped, "He's much too old for her!" My father said, "He's a good man. I've seen him around. He works hard and he could provide for her."

"Provide for her! She's only sixteen!"

The next morning when Annette came down for breakfast, all the fights started.

"Look," Colleen says, pointing to a half-ton truck with G.R. Habbib & Bros., Wholesalers, painted on the side.

"That's it! That's his truck!"

"So what does that mean?"

I look at the modest, two-story home next to where the truck is parked. "He lives there with his parents and one of his brothers," I say. "They all came from Lebanon."

"If his truck is there," Colleen continues, "doesn't that mean he isn't meeting Annette?"

I hadn't thought of that. I was sure the truck wouldn't be there. "Maybe she's in there with him."

We stare at the house. Next door, an old woman comes to the door and calls her cat. Colleen and I hook arms and hurry down the street. When we get to the corner we turn around and come back.

"What could they be doing in there?" Colleen asks.

"Who knows?" I search the lighted windows for clues, but the shades are tightly drawn and the house is silent. Somehow I'd expected something different. Loud music, maybe. Things happening.

"Are you sure they're in there?" Colleen asks the fourth time we walk by the house. Then it occurs to me: there are *two* trucks.

"This must be the brother's truck."

"Oh great," Colleen says. "Let's go home."

Darkness has fallen now, and as we round the corner, we notice that a group of teenagers has gathered under the streetlight in front of Johnny's. Diane and Carolyn are among them, and they are all talking in low tones, as if something important has just happened. When they see us they fall silent.

Carolyn, her eyes narrowed into slits, calls out, "What were you two laughing at before?" A shiver passes through me. "I don't like people laughing at me," she continues, her mouth twisting into a sneer.

"We weren't laughing at you," I answer, swallowing hard. I try not to look at her black and white pants.

"Oh yeah? What was so funny, then?" A dozen pairs of eyes watch us, waiting for the answer.

"Nothing," I say in my most innocent voice, and try to walk past. But the crowd moves, blocking our way. I grab Colleen's arm and steer her into Johnny's, trying to make it look as if we were planning to stop there anyway.

"What are we going to do now?" Colleen whispers. She has a big Adam's apple that bobs up and down when she's nervous; now it's bobbing like crazy.

"Maybe if we stay in here long enough they'll go away."

Colleen follows me up and down the aisles and we study the labels on the canned goods. Johnny, meanwhile, looks at us suspiciously.

After a few minutes, Andy Varner comes in. We know him from last year in grade eight. He hangs around with the boys who smoke.

"Why don't you two go outside," he says, hooking his fingers into his dungaree pockets. "The guys and me would like to see a girl-fight."

Colleen tightens her grip on my arm.

"We don't want to fight," I hear myself saying. My hands feel thick and sweaty.

"Well they do, and we're all waiting for you," he leers. "See you outside."

After he leaves, Johnny calls over, "Do you girls want to buy something?"

"Those kids outside, they're after us!" Colleen blurts out. Johnny looks out the window, then back at us.

"I don't want no trouble," he says. "I think you'd better leave."

"But they'll get us!" I gasp. There's no back door; only a side door with stairs that circle around to the front.

"That's not my business," Johnny says, waving his hands. "I don't want no trouble in here." Colleen's face has turned white and my knees are trembling. Johnny casts an uneasy look out the window again. The crowd has grown steadily larger.

"Look," he says. "If you want to call someone to come get you . . . " He points to the black phone on the edge of the counter.

My father, I think. He could come and get us with the truck. Then I picture the truck full of candy, unguarded; my father's creaking, wheezing body, his swollen red knuckles.

"How about *your* father?" I ask Colleen. They don't have a car but Colleen's house is only a few blocks away and he could come on foot. Colleen's father is a stevedore at the Dockyards; no one would tangle with *him*.

Colleen has to dial the number twice, her fingers are trembling so badly. She blurts out our story to whoever answers. "He's not? Where is he?" Her Adam's apple bobs frantically.

"What? What?" I ask when she hangs up.

"My father had to work tonight. Max said he'd come for us." Colleen's brother Max has always reminded me of a small, raggedy alley dog, with his choppy hair and missing front tooth. Last spring he was thrown out of St. Pat's for fighting; now he works at the Maple Leaf Dairy cleaning ice cream machines.

"He said he'd call the police, too, just in case," Colleen adds. It hadn't occurred to me to call the police.

The store is empty now except for Colleen and me. Johnny, washing glasses behind the counter, glances uneasily out the window. There are probably sixteen kids out there now. Orange tips from burning cigarettes glow like strange, fluorescent insects. Shadowy faces turn toward the store then back to the crowd. Feet shift impatiently.

After what seems like hours but is actually four minutes by the big round clock above the soda fountain, Max comes in, breathing hard. His jaw is set, his face grim. I have never liked him much, so the surge of gratitude I feel for him now astonishes me.

"Stay right close to me when we go out," he says.

When we open the front door, the crowd gets quiet. The white halves of Carolyn's pants gleam in the dark. Max leads us down the stairs, with Colleen and I huddling so close to him we almost trip over his feet.

"Look at the babies!" a female voice calls out. "You think *he's* going to protect you?"

The crowd begins pushing toward us, blocking our way. My legs feel like rubber sticks. Max makes a quick movement, some thing flashes, and the crowd parts.

"Run!" Max yells. He turns to face the crowd, and I see a long silver blade jutting from his right hand.

Colleen and I fly down the street and around the corner, tears soaking our faces, our chests heaving and hurting. Almost at Colleen's house, we notice that Max isn't behind us. "Max!" Colleen yells. "We have to go back and help him!" We turn and start back, though we have no idea what we will do when we get there.

In a few moments we hear sirens; red lights flash over the rooftops. A figure comes hurrying toward us. It's Max. His hands are buried in his jacket pockets and he keeps looking back over his shoulder.

"What happened?" we ask, breathless.

"I ran. Just as the police came."

"Did those guys do anything to you?"

"They couldn't get close enough." His hands move in his pockets, and I wonder which one has the knife in it. I stare at his face, at the twitching muscle over his left cheekbone. It occurs to me now that I have never really looked at Max before, never seen him clearly.

When we get to Colleen's house, we say goodbye.

"You sure you don't want me to go the rest of the way with you?" Max asks.

"It's only a block and a half. Thanks, though." I touch his arm. Somehow I know I'd be all right.

The streets and porches are deserted now — no more children and their wild games, no more spectators; only an eerie, blue-grey light flickering from living room windows. The air feels cooler now, and I sense that the change has already begun. It's like being in a heated room, feeling the cold from outside seeping in through tiny cracks.

When I get home, I slide through the front door into the living room. They are all watching *Kraft Mystery Theatre*: my father hunched in his chair, my mother stretched out on the sofa, Claude and André lying on the floor eating potato chips. For a moment I look at them, shining in their sameness, and I want to take their unknowing and hold it to me. Then someone says, "Where were you?" And what happened comes spilling out of my mouth.

What They Knew

Annette stood at the ironing board, ironing the dress she planned to wear that evening. Their mother, folding clothes at the kitchen table, kept looking over at Annette, her mouth tightening. Nicole tried to hurry up and finish the dishes; she knew what was coming.

"You'll ruin your life this way," her mother said in a low voice.

Annette's shoulders stiffened.

"Eleven years older is too old. You have no idea what it means to live with an older man. Oh, it seems nice at first, 'romantic.' Then they get old and sick and don't care anymore. Wait till you see how romantic that is."

Her mother's eyes were burning into points. Any minute, Nicole thought.

"I'm only trying to help you, Annette, to give you the benefit of my experience, but will you listen? No. You think you know everything."

Annette turned and hissed: "It's *my* life, not yours!" Her mother's face reddened as though she'd been slapped, and words flew through the air like sharpened teeth. *"Miss Smart Alec —" "None of your business —" "You little fool —"*

Nicole slipped out the back door and went around to the front steps to wait it out. When they first started fighting, she had watched them, fascinated. They were like cats — Minou or Solomon with Midnight next door, crouching along the fence line, singing their high-pitched taunts like arias. Eventually one of them would go too far, and the other would be on him in a frenzy of shrieks and hisses.

But these fights had been going on for months. And they weren't funny anymore. An invisible wall had sprung up in their house, with Annette and their father on one side, their mother on the other. Sometimes her mother tried to pull *her* into the battle, but Nicole wanted to stay neutral, like her brothers, who always seemed to be out somewhere when things got sticky.

She listened at the front door. Footsteps hurried up the stairs. Annette's voice shouted, "I don't care what anyone thinks! I'm going to marry Emile next summer as soon as I turn eighteen, whether you like it or not!" A door slammed.

Nicole wasn't sure how she felt about the Annette-Emile business. She liked Emile, but since he'd come along, Annette had changed. She seemed to have gotten smaller, quieter, and all she ever talked about was Emile and getting married.

Last spring, when Annette announced she was quitting school now that she had her grade eleven, her mother had exploded. Her father had said nothing; it didn't seem to bother him at all. And though the battles had raged all summer, Annette hadn't gone back to St. Pat's. Instead, when school started, Annette began working at Zellers full time. Nicole had dropped in to see her after school, and at first she didn't even recognized her: standing behind the counter in her brown uniform, Annette had looked so ordinary.

Once, Annette had wanted to be a scientist. In grade nine, she had gotten a microscope set for Christmas. That winter, she spent hours peering at things on small glass plates, telling Nicole what she saw and explaining what things meant. With her eyes so big and bright behind her glasses, she seemed to know everything. Now, Annette wore her glasses only when Emile wasn't around. Without them, Emile had to lead her around like a blind person.

When the house became completely quiet, Nicole tiptoed up the stairs to her room, pausing at Annette's closed door. She could hear Annette moving around, getting ready. And very faintly, so faintly she had to strain to hear, came the voices of the Everley Brothers, twanging from Annette's small record player: *"never knew what I missed, till I kissed you . . ."*

There was something fishy about this thing with Emile. Even after Annette began sneaking off to dances at the Jubilee with Babbette, she'd still wanted to be a scientist. And last year, when Annette was still in school and working at Zellers only part-time, she bought herself nice things — lipstick, scarves, dresses and shoes. But now that she and Emile planned to get married, she didn't do that anymore. And she didn't talk about what she wanted to be anymore, either. Instead, she put things on layaway: blankets, towels, pots and pans.

From her bedroom window, Nicole watched Emile get out of his car. He wore a freshly pressed dark suit as he always did, and walked up the front steps briskly, confidently, as though he owned all of Halifax. While he stood in the front hall twirling his keys and waiting for Annette, Nicole sat halfway down the stairs studying his broad jaw, his white teeth, the wave of oiled hair piled over his forehead. What was it about him that had made Annette become so queer?

When he noticed her, Emile's mouth stretched into a big smile and he began his usual banter, asking her if she had any boyfriends yet, as if she were still a child.

"I'm just as old as Annette was when she started dating *you*," Nicole said.

He put his hand to his chest and gestured extravagantly. "In that case," he said, drawing the words out importantly, "we'll just have to find you a Lebanese boyfriend. I have several cousins who would love to go out with a nice, pretty girl like you. How would you like that? We could all go out together some night, your sister and I, and you and my cousin, who would be so happy and pleased."

He practically crooned the words, so Nicole knew he was just teasing. It was the same tone of voice he

used when he told her mother how nice she looked, even if she had on an old house dress. "You and Annette look more like sisters than mother and daughter," he'd tell her. Her mother would smile and flutter her eyes, but when Emile and Annette left, she'd say, "The Lebanese are all like that; they don't really mean what they say."

Just as Annette and Emile were about to leave, her father appeared, dressed in his Sunday suit. He'd had his bath and his face glowed pink. The fringe of white hair around his head was carefully combed and he smelled of Bay Rum.

"Can you drop me off at St. Catherine's on the way?" he asked Emile. "There's no place to park my truck, and climbing that hill is hard on my arthritis."

"I'd be glad to, Mr. LeBlanc," Emile said, no longer crooning. When he talked to her father, his voice sounded different. It was as though they shared a secret, something men knew but women didn't.

Nicole and her mother watched the threesome walk down the front steps and get into Emile's car. Her father eased himself in, lifting his legs slowly. Under his left arm he carried a box of black licorice. Her father went to confession once a month, on a Saturday evening. Afterward, he went to see his sister, Tante Matilde, who lived a block from the church.

"Muriel must be constipated again," her mother said. "I don't know why they don't just buy that girl a laxative. No wonder your father's candy business is in trouble — all the stuff he gives away!"

Nicole thought of her cousin Muriel, a large, somber-looking girl, three years older than Annette. She pictured Muriel lowering herself into a cushioned chair, reaching for the licorice twists, and grinding them one by one with her solemn jaws. Halfway through the box, Muriel's eyelids suddenly lift and a churning, roiling sound comes from her belly. She bolts for the bathroom, her jaws still grinding.

Nicole began to laugh. Her mother looked at her, and as if she were reading her mind, began laughing too.

"Poor Muriel," her mother said. "On top of everything else."

They stood at the door for a few minutes, looking out. Then her mother sighed.

"What do *you* think? Do you think I should give them my permission, let them get married now?"

"I don't know," Nicole answered, looking down.

"Your father thinks we should," her mother continued. "He says Emile's a fine man and there's no reason to stop them. Of course your father doesn't see anything wrong with anything as long as it doesn't affect him. But seventeen is so young. She needs to meet other people."

Nicole didn't completely understand why her mother was so opposed. Everyone got married sometime. A lot of girls she knew were planning their weddings even though they didn't even have boyfriends yet. Yet her mother never mentioned the funny changes in Annette. All her mother ever said was that Annette was too young, or needed to meet other people.

"Annette's been going out with Emile since she was fifteen," Nicole said, picking her words carefully. "Even if you don't let them get married, that doesn't mean she'll meet anyone else."

Her mother was silent for a moment. "I hope you won't be as foolish as your sister," she said, giving Nicole a hard look.

The next day, when they all sat down for the big Sunday dinner, Nicole's father said, "Your cousin Kay is doing well at the Mount. She's a smart girl; she's planning to be a mathematician."

Her mother's face stiffened. It always did when her father mentioned Tante Matilde or her daughters. Kay was the same age as Annette, and unlike Muriel, bone thin. Her glasses were as thick as the bottom of Big 8 bottles.

Her father looked at them all expectantly, as if he were waiting for them to say: Isn't that wonderful. Instead, her mother said, "It would be nice if you took half as much interest in your own children as you do in Matilde's."

Her father's face turned dark red. "Can't I say anything at all about them without you getting jealous?"

Nicole felt her stomach tighten. Why did they always have to fight at mealtime? At least this one wasn't about Annette and Emile.

"Jealous! Don't make me laugh! Why you are more interested in those two homely girls than in your own daughters who are beautiful as well as smart, and your own sons, I'll never know. She must have some power over you, that woman."

"That's ridiculous, Claire! Power over me indeed. I don't know why you dislike Matilde so much. She's a fine woman."

"A fine woman! A fine woman invites her brother over time after time and never invites his wife and children. That's a fine woman all right."

"You know very well you wouldn't go even if she did invite you!"

Her mother didn't reply. She had tired of the quarrel. Nicole could tell by her sigh, by the way she told André to pass the gravy. There was a silence now. Even Claude, usually so full of jokes, chewed quietly on his chicken leg. No one seemed to know what to say, so Nicole announced cheerfully, "I've decided to be an archeologist, like Schliemann. He discovered Troy. We're studying all about it in my classics class."

Her mother looked up. "That's wonderful, dear."

"Aren't they the ones who dig up mummies and steal their loot?" Claude asked.

"It's much more involved than that," Nicole said, giving him an icy look. "You have to know all kinds of history and science and mythology, so you know what things mean."

"Maybe you can win a scholarship to Dalhousie or to the Mount like your cousin Kay," her mother said, staring pointedly at their father. "After all, you won one for the Convent School, so it's quite possible."

"What do you think, Dad?" Nicole watched her father's mouth. She pictured him wearing the same funny smile he wore when he talked about her cousins, telling Tante Matilde: Nicole plans to be an archeologist.

But her father kept eating, as if he hadn't heard her.

"What do you think, Dad?" she asked again.

"Well," her father said. "I don't know if it's a good idea for you to think about going to university."

"But I might be able to get a scholarship, like Mom says. Then we wouldn't have to worry about paying for it."

Her father put down his fork and looked at her.

"You don't need all that education, Nicole. Don't you see? You'd be taking the place of a man who could use that education to get a good job to support his family."

"That's rubbish!" her mother interjected. "This is 1959, not 1940."

Nicole felt a hard spot forming in her chest. "How can you say that, Dad? What about Kay? You think it's fine for her." Perhaps what her mother said was true. Perhaps her father did care more about his nieces than his own children.

"Kay is no beauty," her father said softly. "You know that. She'll probably never get married. She needs an education because she'll have to support herself. But you'll find a husband with no trouble at all. Like Annette."

At this point her mother burst in saying something about having to support him as well as herself, and if she hadn't gone to Normal School in Truro they'd be in big trouble right now. But Nicole wasn't listening any more. She stared at the food on her plate which looked suddenly greasy and unappealing.

"Men!" her mother said. "Don't listen to him, Nicole. You can be anything you want. Husband or no husband. I'm glad at least one of my daughters is interested in making something of herself!"

Annette stopped chewing for a moment, but didn't look up.

Later, after the dishes were done and her mother and father had retired to their separate bedrooms to rest, Nicole pushed open Annette's bedroom door. Annette was counting her money. "Great dinner we had, eh?" Annette said, looking up. On her desk were little piles of dollar bills and the notebook in which she kept track of her layaways.

"I really do want to be an archeologist," Nicole said. She wasn't sure that she really did, but she wanted to hear what Annette thought.

"So do it," Annette said. "If that's what you want." She went over to the bed and pulled out one of the boxes she kept underneath. Inside were a set of stainless steel cutlery for six, a pair of sheets and pillow cases with pink flowers, and a blue teapot. She picked up the teapot and stroked it.

"Don't *you* want to be anything anymore?" Nicole blurted out.

"I want to be married. I want to be Mrs. Emile Habbib, that's what I want to be," Annette said.

"You used to want to be a scientist, remember? Can't you be a scientist and be married?"

Annette looked at her as though she were six years old and very stupid. "Of course you can, but it takes years to be a scientist. You have to study and study, and it's hard to be married while you do that. Anyway, I don't want to be a scientist anymore." She pushed the box back under the bed and returned to the desk. In the back of her notebook she had a long list called Things We'll Need. She wrote: laundry hamper.

"How come you don't want to be a scientist anymore?"

Annette puckered her lips. "It's too complicated to explain."

One Saturday evening, a few weeks later, Nicole answered the phone and heard a heavily-accented male voice asking for An — . At first she thought he wanted André. But the voice sounded too old to belong to one of André's friends.

"Do you mean Annette? Do you want to speak to Annette? I'm sorry but she's out."

"Who are *you*?" he wanted to know.

"I'm her sister, Nicole."

His name was Jon, and he was a merchant marine. After asking him to repeat himself several times, Nicole learned that he had met Annette at the Jubilee when his ship was last in Halifax. If Annette was busy, he said, maybe she, Nicole would like to go to a movie with him. They could still catch the nine o'clock show.

Nicole hesitated for a moment, then said yes.

"I'll meet you in front of the Oxford Theater in an hour," she said.

Nicole searched her closet for something suitable to wear. If only Annette were around to give her some advice! She couldn't ask her mother; her mother would almost certainly forbid her to go. She thought of her father and wondered what he would say. He approved of Emile, but somehow, this didn't seem like the same thing.

When she came downstairs, she pulled her coat on quickly so her mother wouldn't notice she was wearing her good brown wool skirt with the matching paisley blouse.

"I'm taking the trolley over to Meredith's," she called into the kitchen. "We might go to a movie."

"Okay," her mother called back. "Don't stay out too late."

In the trolley, Nicole found herself tying the fingers of her gloves into knots. How would they recognize each other? She pictured someone who looked like Emile waiting for her, with Emile's big, welcoming grin. The few boys her own age she had gone out with now struck her as silly and childish, like her brothers. Jon was a man. He was connected to Annette's world, to the things Annette knew. Looking out into the night, Nicole felt that a great secret was about to unfold.

The man waiting in front of the Oxford Theater scrutinizing every passing female did not look much like Emile. He was short, barely as tall as Nicole, and instead of wearing a nice suit like Emile, he wore a thick, navy blue fisherman's sweater over a dark shirt and dark pants.

He steered her by her elbow into a seat in one of the back rows. Nicole studied his face in furtive glances. He had an olive complexion and a square jaw like Emile's, but that's where the similarity ended. His eyebrows were thick and black, and the lower half of his face was sooty-looking. His hands, when they touched hers, felt rough, like heavy rope. He smelled of garlic.

"Are you Lebanese?" she whispered as soon as they were seated.

"No, I am from Romania," he said. He said something else, too, but his accent was so thick she couldn't understand him. She nodded, pretending she did.

No sooner had the lights gone down when she felt his arm inch around her shoulder. She wanted to say, *You don't even know me,* but part of her was curious to see what else would happen.

It was a Doris Day movie, *Pillow Talk.* When she turned to make a comment, she found that he was not watching the movie at all; his dark eyes were watching *her,* his face hovering only a few inches away from hers. She tried to act as if this were perfectly normal and turned back to the movie. But she found it hard to concentrate, feeling his eyes on her, the pressure of his arm around her shoulder pulling her closer. When she turned to protest, his mouth suddenly clamped on hers and he pressed his hard tongue past her teeth and into her mouth. She struggled to free herself. His tongue was thick and slimy, like a slug.

When she managed to wriggle free, he settled back into his chair looking pleased, as if he had accomplished something. Nicole wiped her mouth with the back of her hand and shuddered. How dare he take advantage of her like that! Though she felt his arm slide around her shoulders again, she kept herself rigid and stared straight ahead at the screen until the movie was over.

On the way out he took her by the elbow and, blinking and smiling, suggested they go for a drink someplace. The throng of movie goers was spreading out across the street toward the cluster of waiting trolleys.

"I have to go home now," Nicole said. She broke away from him and half ran across the street. Only when she was safely in the trolley did she dare look back. He was standing on the corner where she had left him, staring at the bus with a forlorn, puzzled face.

All the way home, Nicole thought about what had happened. To think she had lied to her mother, too, for *this*! And she would have to lie again when her mother asked her if she and Meredith had had a good time. She longed to wash her face, rinse out her mouth, pretend that the whole evening had never happened. But she also wanted to tell someone, to hear her own voice telling it, to see the face of someone listening.

After dinner the next day, Nicole went into Annette's room, bursting with the need to tell. Annette was at her desk again, making notes in her layaway book. Nicole sat on the edge of Annette's bed, wondering how to begin. She was sure some filament of shared memory, shared dreams, still joined them, but somehow she couldn't seem to find it. If only she could, then maybe she could grab hold of it and reel out the old Annette, like a fish. The old Annette would know what it all meant, would help her make sense of it.

"You should see the beautiful dinette set I saw yesterday," Annette said. "If Emile likes it, I'm going to put it on layaway."

"Where will you put it when you get it paid off?" Nicole asked. "I don't think it'll fit under the bed."

"Very funny," Annette said. "I'll be eighteen in May; I haven't told anybody yet, but Emile and I have set the date for June 6th. It'll probably take me that long to pay for it, anyway."

"If you were a scientist you'd make a lot of money and you could buy all those things without having to use layaway."

Annette gave her a hard look. "Of course I would. And if I were a man I'd make even more. But I'm not, am I?"

"What do you mean if you were a man you'd make even more?"

"Every one knows men are paid more than women."

"That can't be right," Nicole protested.

"Yes it is. You can ask Mom."

Nicole felt a funny tingling up and down her spine. "But that's not fair! Why would they do that?"

"It's like Dad says, I guess. They figure men have families to support."

"But women do too! Look at Mom."

"Listen, I don't like it either," Annette said, "but that's the way it is." She opened her desk drawer and pulled out a small pile of dollar bills neatly bound with a rubber band.

"But why don't women object? Why would they let them get away with it?"

"That's just the way it is," Annette said again, shrugging.

How could Annette just sit there and not let it bother her? Annette who used to be so strong, so smart . . . So that was it! Something happened to girls when they became women. Something clicked in them, like a switch, and they became ordinary, not themselves. Then men could take advantage of them. She thought of her father and Emile and all the other men she knew, the tone of voice they used when they spoke to each other. *They all knew!* Nicole felt a cold wind blow through her. She watched Annette quietly counting her money, the money that would be more if she were a man. She felt a sudden, ferocious urge to take Annette and shake her, to shake and shake her until the old Annette tumbled out. Annette took a five-dollar bill from the pile, folded it, and slipped it into an envelope marked "Small Appliances."

Circle of Light

He woke, the darkness thick around him. He could hear the crickets outside, the jangling of their legs like a symphony of Jews' harps. His father had brought him one sixty-two years ago, when he was eight, brought it all the way from England in the great clipper ship. He could still remember the sails, billowing in the wind, the sudden light, the spray of the sea. He had been the first to see it hovering on the horizon like a ghost. They had all gone down to the wharf, his mother, his brother, other women and children from the village. How he had strained to remember his father's face, the feel of his scratchy whiskers, the blue of his eyes. His father had been gone so long! They had said the rosary for him every night — *Sainte Marie, Mère de Dieu* — to Ave Maris Stella, who watched over the sea. And suddenly his father was there, lifting him up, smelling of salt and pipe tobacco, bigger than he remembered, with huge calloused hands. Hands that held his gift from England, wrapped in a red check handkerchief — the Jews' harp with its twangy, cricket leg.

    He couldn't have slept long. A short burst of sleep, that was all, a short descent into blackness. His sleep was dreamless these nights; dreams hovered over his waking hours instead. The house was still. Claire, in her bed in the room above — was that her turning in her sleep? And Annette and Nicole, in the two rooms next to hers, curled against their pillows like dolls, a brown-haired, brown-eyed doll, and a blond, blue-eyed one. No. That wasn't right. Annette was gone now. She slept in her husband's house. And Nicole, she would soon be gone, off to the States, now that she had her scholarship. He wouldn't think of that. He'd think instead of Claude and André asleep in their bunks, their gangly limbs draped over the sides, their mouths half-open, like the window they sometimes crept through when the rest of the household slept. He'd caught them at it once, on his way to empty his bladder. Their beds were rumpled but empty, the curtain flapping against the sill where the screen had been.

    Where did they go? What drew them? It wasn't girls. Beardless, they blushed and fumbled when Nicole brought her girl friends home. What did they do out there in the darkness? They shrugged their shoulders when he asked them. Nothing, they said. We just hang around and look at things. Sometimes Pete and Ducky go with us. We talk.

He knew that the darkness itself drew them. The night air, suddenly chill. The silence. The way the city closed itself up like a flower. At night, you could look at things from the outside. See the shapes of things. They'd told him they wouldn't sneak out anymore, but he knew they would. And did. He hadn't told Claire.

He felt a swelling in his bladder, an urgent gathering of liquid. It was time. Twice, sometimes three times a night, he had to get up. He padded down the hall toward the bathroom, pausing at the door of the boys' room. Tonight they slept. The bottom of the top bunk sagged with André's body; Claude, below, snuffled through a perpetually blocked nose. When he reached the bathroom, he did not turn on the light. His eyes were accustomed to the dark now, and the light from Mrs. Smith's back porch filtered through the window. Everyone slept except him, and he knew he would not sleep again for some time.

He went into the living room and lowered himself into his chair. He turned on the reading lamp, creating only a small circle of light, but everything changed. A moment ago, he had been part of the darkness, one with it. Now, he was outside the darkness, looking in. He picked up his book, *The Perennial Philosophy*, by Aldous Huxley. For days, now, he had been studying it. Perhaps it had something to tell him; he had felt that it might the moment he'd opened its covers. Now he held it, looking from the light into the darkness. Even the crickets sounded different, heard from inside the light. Their song was flatter, less mysterious, as though separated from him not just by a screen, but by a wall of glass.

All his life he had been looking at things through a wall of glass, it seemed to him now. A wall of glass that separated, that let you see without entering, see without touching. The surface of things. Images moving, hiding their mysteries.

Something thunked against the screen beside him. A huge moth hurled itself toward the light, the light it couldn't reach. Again and again it came, and with it a few of its brethren, all slamming themselves against the screen, frenzied, insistent, caught up in the motion itself. Like the waves of young men who had swarmed the hills in France, hurling themselves toward the front, where they burst into flames. Like the moths, that time with the lamp, when he was a boy. He would play his Jews' harp in the evenings, sitting on the front porch of the big white house, after the others had gone to bed. Sometimes he sneaked the oil lamp from the kitchen table and brought it outside. The moths would come out of the night and rush toward the flame, beating themselves wildly against the glass chimney. Their wings, yellow and orange and brown and blue and cream like the petals of exotic flowers, left a fine, powdery trace. Once he had raised the chimney a few inches, just to see what would happen, and watched those powdery wings incinerate.

What you want sometimes kills you, he had learned then. And what had he wanted? *Something*, something that had eluded him, something for which he, too, had slammed himself against life. He couldn't remember what it was, exactly. A nameless yearning had filled him, had driven him from job to job, from place to place. Something he was looking for. Something he wanted to find out. For a while he had been distracted, first by the demands of his family — a young wife, children a half-century different — then by the rumbling and shrieking of his joints and his lower back. But it was still there, that voice with its large question. He heard it at night, now, in the darkness, that small voice from somewhere, asking the old, wordless question.

He felt an insect ping against his head, so he shut off the lamp. The darkness wrapped itself around him like a shawl. In a few moments his eyes adjusted, and he began to see more clearly, without the lamp. The corners of the room seemed lighter, like secrets come out of hiding. Suddenly the room filled with light again, for just a second, startling him. Surely, he had imagined it. But no, it happened again. The room, filled with yellow light for less than a second, then became darker than before. Was this one of his waking dreams? Then he saw the pale, florescent green body as it flew around him. He had gathered a whole canning jar full of them once, when he was a boy, thinking he could read all night by their light. He leaned back in his chair and watched it, the small circle of light appearing in various parts of the room, blinking on and off like a persistent question.

Evangeline

Nicole wasn't sure she wanted to go, but not going meant staying home with her father and her brothers.

"It'll be nice, Nicole," her mother urged. "Everyone is proud of you; they want to see you. And Grand-mère is getting so old; you might not have a chance to see her again."

This was true. Now that Nicole was going away to the States, who knew what would happen?

"Besides, it's just for two days and one night. We'll leave here early on Saturday morning. With the new highway, we should be there by eleven."

André and Claude had used their paper routes as an excuse not to come along, but Nicole knew that wasn't the real reason. "It's boring there," they'd said. Earlier that summer they had hauled home an old car;

now they spent every available moment trying to make it run.

Emile had borrowed his cousin's new 1963 Buick for the trip. It was light blue and shiny, and without the boys, there was plenty of room in the back seat for her and her mother. Annette sat in front, holding the baby.

"He's Grandmère's first great-grandchild," Annette said, bouncing the baby on her knee. "We have to show you off, don't we?" He had a thick shock of black hair like Emile's, and Annette had combed it into a glossy curl.

"It's so nice to be traveling in this car," her mother said. "That old truck was awful to ride in."

"You should get yourself a car," Emile said. "A nice little car to drive yourself to school. Then you could go anywhere you want, whenever you want."

Her mother laughed. "I don't know how to drive. Besides, cars cost a lot of money. Where would I find money for a car?"

"There are used ones that don't cost too much. And it's not hard to drive. I could teach you."

Emile seemed like part of the family now. He was always helping out, now that her father didn't do much of anything anymore. Once last winter, when the furnace broke down, Emile had come over and fixed it. He'd fixed the screen door, too, after Claude had crashed through it. Her mother and Annette got along fine these days; it was hard to remember the old fights.

Nicole looked out the car window at the passing fields and small orchards. It was nice to be going to the country again. She hadn't seen her aunts and uncles and Grandmère in three whole years. It was as if a part of her had gotten lost. Where had it gone?

When they arrived, Tante Yolande met them at the door in her apron. Oncle Louie came out from the barn and they stood in the front of the house for a few minutes, hugging each other and admiring the baby. Oncle Louie's cheeks were red and he smelled of chewing tobacco. He had always been Nicole's favourite uncle. Emile shook their hands, saying *"Bonjour,"* with a Lebanese accent.

They went into the kitchen, where Grandmère waited for them in her rocking chair. She looked older and frailer than ever. She was eighty-four now, and spent most of her days in her rocking chair, looking out the window. Beyond the road and the grassy fields, the blue of Saint Mary's Bay shimmered against the horizon.

Tante Yolande's big kitchen was much the same as Nicole remembered — the wood stove on one side, the long table with eight chairs on the other. A low cot with a few cushions stood against a far wall. Faucets for hot and cold running water had replaced the pump, but the wooden sink with the white enamelled basin remained. Behind the stove a door led to the pantry where the milk-separating machine was kept, and the pie safe, where Tante Yolande had always stored her rolls and pies and gingerbread. Nicole had a sudden urge to go in and look, but thought it would be impolite. Perhaps later. The kitchen smelled of fresh bread and crisping pork fat. Tante Yolande had made a huge *pâté à la râpure* in honor of their visit.

Tante Yolande's sons were all at work, but Tante Élise and Oncle Roland soon arrived from across the street, trailed by a few of their younger children. There was a flurry of activity while Oncle Louie brought in extra chairs from the living room. After they all settled down there was a moment of silence, as if they had all become suddenly shy.

"So, you had a good trip?" Oncle Roland began.

Yes, they had.

"And Charles, he's well?"

Her aunts and uncles spoke to them in English. This, Nicole supposed, was in deference to Emile who had forgotten most of the French he had learned in Lebanon. They probably thought she and Annette had forgotten it, too. She knew they were used to switching back and forth, speaking English to strangers, French among themselves, but their English sounded awkward, as if the words were sharp and hurt their mouths.

Nicole listened to Tante Yolande say something to Grandmère. Her words were twangy, familiar, reminding Nicole of all the summers she had spent here. "Country French," Mother McGuire at school had called it when Nicole had first spoken that way in French class. Humiliated, she had practiced and practiced speaking the other way; now she spoke "good French," like the Parisians.

"So, you're off to the States." Oncle Louie said, smiling and nodding at her. "Your mudder wrote to us about your scholarship."

"Yes," she said. She thought of all the summers she had followed him around. His trick with the cow's milk. How he once told her he wished she were his daughter so he'd have her around to tease all the time. Now he was speaking to her in English, as though she were a stranger. If she answered him in French, he'd know she still spoke it; but she couldn't bring herself to say the words the twangy way he said them.

His big rough hands dangled awkwardly over his knees. How she had loved watching those hands with their thick, blunt fingers, as they milked the cows, chopped wood, or pitched hay. Once, when she was eight or nine, he had led his big work horse all around the barnyard while she perched on its back, pretending to be Elizabeth Taylor in *National Velvet*.

"*Ta Grandmère* went to the States when she was young," he continued. "Just like you. She was a governess in Boston for nearly ten years."

Nicole stared at Grandmère — frail old Grandmère.

"In dose days young people went to Boston to look for work. You didn't need papers and permits and all dose tings," he continued.

Her father had gone to Boston, too, when he was young. And to New York and Pittsburgh and other places. Sometimes she felt nervous and queer about going so far away. Yet Grandmère and her father had both done that, and long ago, when journeys were harder and took longer.

She tried to picture Grandmère as a young woman. Grandmère by herself, going to the States. She was only four feet ten inches and weighed eighty pounds. Her hands were thin and sinewy, like chicken feet. Grand-

mère had always seemed old and frail, even in Nicole's earliest memories. Once, when she and Annette were five and six, they had looked at her in awe and said, *"La Grandmère est veille, veille, veille."* Grandmère would have been sixty-nine or seventy then. The same age as her father was now, she realized suddenly.

She looked at Grandmère sitting in her rocker with a knitted shawl over her legs, smiling and talking to Annette and the baby. Her mother and Tante Yolande were checking the *pâté à la râpure* to see if it was ready. The kitchen was busy and bright, full of good smells and cheerful talk. She thought of her father back home, sitting alone in the living room, in his old chair. He would probably open a can of beans for himself and the boys. Then the boys would disappear somewhere.

At noon Pierre came home. Her other cousins, Jean Paul and Dennis, worked in Yarmouth, too far to come home at noon, but Pierre worked in Meteghan, at the fish processing plant. His, however, was only a summer job; this fall he would go to the Collège Sainte-Anne in Church Point, the only college in Nova Scotia that taught in French.

"He could have gone to Moncton or Montréal," Oncle Louie said. "But we thought we'd keep him close to home so we could keep an eye on him."

"I hear you won a big scholarship," Pierre said, flashing his dimples at Nicole. "Congratulations."

"Thank you," she said, both embarrassed and pleased that he mentioned it. He spoke English with the same thick accent the others used. She couldn't imagine him going to a school where they spoke English all the time. He seemed so much a part of this world.

Pierre went over to the basin to wash his hands. Nicole studied his dark hair and eyes, his rosy cheeks. She remembered the summer she had been Evangeline, and he Gabriel for the Acadian festival. Did he remember it too? She was only ten then, but what a crush she had had on him! He was still better looking than most of the boys she knew in Halifax, she noted.

As she set the plates on the table, Nicole heard Tante Yolande whisper to her mother: *"S'il ne l'aime pas, je peux lui préparer des oeufs."* Emile. Tante Yolande was worried that he wouldn't like *pâté à la râpure*. It hadn't occurred to her that someone might not like it. When they sat down, Emile put a big forkful of it in his mouth and made agreeable noises. "The traditional dish of the Acadians," he said with great fanfare. "It's very good. *Très très bon.*" Yolande beamed.

After they had eaten and the dishes were washed, they went over to Tante Isabelle's house to spend the rest of the afternoon and to have supper. Annette and Emile and the baby would spend the night there, and Nicole and her mother would return to Oncle Louie's house to sleep.

Tante Isabelle was even more impressed with her scholarship than the others. She fussed over Nicole and talked about what a great honor it was. Oncle Hébert took them out to look at the hen house, the new rabbit cage, his huge raspberry patch. He joked about the time the rooster had chased her and Annette around the yard when they were little. Her aunts and uncles had always seemed so smart, so funny. They seemed different, now, speaking English; not like she remembered, but diminished somehow, speaking in that slow, halting way.

On the way back to Oncle Louie's house, Nicole and her mother stopped in front of a broken down house.

"It's hard to believe, but we once spent part of a summer in that house," her mother said.

"Is that the house we rented?" Nicole asked, staring at the drooping porch and broken windows. The sun had gone down, and the house stood in silhouette against a pink and peach horizon.

"Yes," her mother said.

They had rented the house so they could all stay together instead of having to stay a few here and a few there, among the aunts and uncles, as they usually did. The house was shabby and old then; now it looked uninhabitable. And yet they had been happy there. She remembered that summer clearly, the long days playing in the fields with her cousins, the afternoons at the shore, the salty wind, the blue blue sky. They had all spoken French that summer. Even André and Claude, who barely knew how to say *"Comment ça va"* any more. How much they had loved coming here! How could they have forgotten?

Later, after Nicole and her mother had settled themselves in bed, her mother said, "It's nice to be here, isn't it?"

"Yes," Nicole said. It was pitch dark, unlike their house in Halifax, where the streetlight shone right into her bedroom window. It felt good being in the dark with the window open, the cool night air drifting in, smelling of hay. They could hear the soft lowing of cattle, the occasional cluck of a restive hen. As she lay there in the dark, Nicole found herself remembering the summer she'd been Evangeline. She had felt like a celebrity then, too, riding along on the float with Pierre. *L'Acadie — 1755-1955,* the sign had read. Two hundred years since the Great Deportation.

She thought of all the stories she had grown up with, stories of the Acadians who had been forced to leave Nova Scotia so long ago, how they had watched from the boats while the English burned their villages. They would have been people like her aunts and uncles and her cousins — country people — who loved their land, their animals, their quiet lives along the Bay. It pierced her to think of them, forced to go to places where they were not wanted, where no one knew them, where no one spoke their language. No wonder they had wanted to come back! She pictured them — a whole people dispersed, ragged bands of them regrouping, going home. She tried to imagine what it must have been like to travel those great distances by foot, pulling rough carts with the few belongings they'd managed to acquire. What they must have gone through! And yet they had made it. Her ancestors. They had come back.

A century and a half later, Grandmère and her father had repeated that old pattern: they had left Nova Scotia — *l'Acadie* — and then returned. People used to do that all the time, according to Oncle Louie. It was as if worn paths stretched between Nova Scotia and the New England States, paths forged by the feet of those first exiled, then returning, Acadians. Staring up into the darkness she could almost see those paths, troops of Acadians going back and forth. Soon she would join that ancient migration, following Evangeline, just as Grandmère and her father had.

And how would it be there, in the States? How long would she be away? Grandmère had been gone ten long years before she returned. And her father . . . ? She didn't know. And Evangeline . . . Evangeline had never come back. Could that happen to her? She shuddered. There was no way of knowing.

All summer she had tried to imagine what her life in the States would be like. Now she thought of the moment of leaving. Had her father and Grandmère faced the journey with this same bright eagerness, this same piercing regret? Had they, too, wondered if they would ever come back?

She thought of Evangeline wandering around the American States searching for Gabriel. Though she had never returned, Evangeline had never forgotten. The memory of home had burned in her — Gabriel, the cozy hearth, *L'Acadie* in happier times — and she had carried that bright flame with her forever.

The next morning at Mass in the big Catholic Church in Meteghan, Nicole felt the villagers staring at them, wondering who they were. The sermon was in French, and though she couldn't understand it all, she understood most of it. Years ago, when she'd sat on the float, the Monseigneur had talked about language and religion. That's what made them Acadian, he'd said. She looked around at the faces of the parishioners; they all looked like variations of her aunts and uncles and cousins. They all shared the same ancestors: Acadians who had come back.

After Mass a woman came up to her mother. *"C'est Claire à Madeline à Basil, n'est ce pas?"* she asked. Yes, her mother responded in French, explaining that she was visiting with her two daughters and her son-in-law. She pushed Nicole forward. "This is my youngest daughter. She's going away to the States. She won a big scholarship there."

The woman's eyes got big. Did her daughter speak French, the woman wanted to know.

"Oui, je parle français," Nicole heard herself saying.

The woman's face lit up. *"C'est bon ça."* So many young people didn't care about their language anymore, she lamented. How nice to find one who did. And one who was smart, too! They spoke a little more, Nicole answering all the woman's questions in French. It was Parisian French, but what did it matter how she said the words? They were French words, and that's what counted.

Oncle Louie stood a little to one side waiting for them. He caught Nicole's eye. "So you haven't forgotten your French after all," he said, addressing her in French for the first time.

"*Non,*" she replied and winked, as if she had played a trick on him. *"Je m'en souviens."*

She would never forget, she resolved. She would remember everything. Always. She could feel it burning in her, that small, bright flame.

Part 2

Return

Often, now, I wake in the night to the distant whistle of a train, and for a moment it is the deep, mournful call of the foghorns off the coast of Nova Scotia. And the memory of those foggy days leaps at me whole, those days when downtown Halifax smelled of salt and fish, and it seemed as though the sea had swallowed the city, and we would be suspended forever in a limbo of sunless brine. Now the morning fog that hangs in the hollows of these Virginia hills, that rises through the trees in little, wispy fingers, that hovers eerily over the river, holds that memory taut — keeps it from slipping back to its old, hidden place.

I do not know why I am so haunted. Those were years of hardship, struggle, aching joy; Halifax a place I could hardly wait to leave. Perhaps it is the passing of my fortieth birthday, the taking stock, the confusion of self that comes from a life now lived in equal parts there and away from there. I only know that I must return.

My mother, who has been pressing me for a long time to come, is elated. "I can hardly wait," she says, warbling into the phone. "Four years is much too long between visits."

Soon I am sorting through my drawers and closets: what to bring for walks, for picnics, for the visit to my old Convent School. I pack something for all kinds of weather, for I no longer remember what June is like there.

The trip is a long one, with hours between flights to wander through airports. Hours to tumble through memories from the first half of my life, memories that now cascade around me like rain. Though I leave my house at seven in the morning, it is ten at night before I reach the Halifax airport. As I walk through the terminal gates I see them: my mother and Sammy, her long time friend; my brother, Pascal, and his wife, Vera; my sister, Jeannette, and her son, Louis. For a moment they are framed there, their faces, eager, expectant. They have come to claim me. Watching them, I feel a piercing sense of separateness: all these years, their lives have gone on without me.

Sammy is the first to spot me, waving a wiry arm, and suddenly there is a flurry of excited cries, of hugs and kisses, of how-wonderful-you-look. We smile and pat each other and balance on the balls of our feet, measuring the differences since we last met. Louis has grown a foot since I last saw him and now towers over my sister, who seems shorter than before, her face and body becoming more and more like my mother's. It is the old, shared memories that bind us — and the kinship — for in many ways our present selves are strangers.

"You talk like a Yankee now," my brother grouses.

"Down there they say I talk like a Canuck," I return, tweaking his beard, grown long and luxuriant since our last meeting. We go to the airport cafeteria where we drink mugs of hot tea and make rough plans for the days ahead: when and where to have our traditional lobster boil, which dinner I will eat at whose house, what I would like to do while I am there. Then the others return to their homes, and my mother and I return to hers.

Now begins a careful journey through each room of my childhood home. My mother follows me, touching my arm and hand, "See, those are the new drapes I got since you were here last. And I had that chair recovered. Do you like it?" "Yes," I say, "the house looks great." The living room is bright and attractive, not at all like the shabby room I remember from my girlhood. Thick carpets now cover the linoleum floors my mother used to scrub and wax on her hands and knees every Saturday.

Next comes my father's old bedroom, the one that sometimes haunts my dreams with its cluttered dresser and dusty piles of books, its smell of old age and the cheap cologne my father used to mask the smell of urine, after he became incontinent. But every trace of the old room and my father is gone. Now it is a cozy den, where my mother keeps the mementoes of her travels. The tiny bedroom next to the bathroom, where we four children once slept, is now my mother's dressing room. I stare at the two dressers and single bed that now fill the room. How did we all fit? Yet I was eleven before there was money enough to build an upstairs, with rooms for Jeannette and me, and my mother.

Except for a few new things, a few rearrangements, everything is much the same as it was the last time I visited, four years before. How is it, then, this is not what I remembered? Why do I feel vaguely disappointed?

We pause at the kitchen door. The old wringer-washer no longer dominates the kitchen; it has long ago been replaced by an automatic now in the basement. I flash on the many, many Saturday mornings my mother and Jeannette and I stood by the wringer, feeding load after load of sheets and long underwear through its hungry rollers.

"Do you remember the old washing machine, Mom? I'll never forget hanging the clothes on the line in winter. I thought my fingers would fall off from the cold!"

"Gosh, yes!" She shudders. "Sometimes the clothes were still frozen stiff when we brought them in at night. Too bad I didn't have these nice appliances when you children were little." She pauses for a moment, then adds, "Remember the old oil stove? We'd scrub it for hours with steel wool to get it clean."

"I sure do!"

But it is hard to picture now, with the sparkling, white electric stove that stands in its place. I try to recall the winter mornings, when my father got up at six to light the stove, so it would warm the kitchen before the rest of us arose. When he called from the bottom of the stairs, Jeannette and I would rush down from our frigid room, open the oven door, and hold out the bottoms of our heavy flannel nightgowns to let the warm air flow under them. None of that remains now. Not a trace in this bright, modern kitchen.

My mother stands beside me, hugging my arm, thinking her own thoughts, while I think mine.

"Oh, I have something special for you!" She draws me to the counter and opens a canister of home-made date squares and molasses cookies.

"These were your favorites when you were little," she says smiling. I grin, grab a handful of cookies, and give her a hug.

"It's nice to have you back," she says.

"It's nice to *be* back."

In my old bedroom upstairs, only the white wrought iron bed remains unchanged — the bed that came from D'Escousse, my father's Cape Breton home, the bed that saw my transformation into womanhood. On the pillow I find a sheet of paper with a poem my mother has written to welcome me home. Though it is almost embarrassingly sentimental, it is heartfelt, and I am touched.

Later, while I am lying there remembering the old sufferings of this house, my mother comes in, in her nightgown, to kiss me good night. Always, I remember, it was this way. She would come up carrying a glass of water and pause at my room to open my window, tuck me in, and kiss me good night.

"Aren't you going to open my window too?" I ask as she begins to leave.

"Oh, do you want it opened?"

"No, but you always used to open it, whether I wanted it opened or not. Remember?"

She laughs, opens my window, and goes to her own room. It is very late by now, and I fall asleep instantly.

The next morning I awaken to sun streaming through the windows. For a moment I am jarred. I had expected fog, or overcast skies, for this is what I remember most. The air is cool and fresh, full of bird song.

Downstairs, my mother is preparing French toast and sausages. We take our plates outside and sit at the picnic table on the tiny patio, both new since I left home.

"The yard always looks so small now, when I come back," I remark. "And so lush." I remember scrubby weeds and patches of bare earth.

"Look how big your apple tree has grown," my mother says. "Remember when you planted that apple core? You were eleven, and we all laughed at you, saying it would never grow. Now just look at it!"

I had forgotten the apple core soon after planting it, and the small seedling that miraculously sprouted went unnoticed for a long time. After I left home my mother discovered it and quietly watched it grow. It bloomed for the first time well into my adult years; now, each spring, my mother reports on its progress. I am pleased that she cherishes the tree and the memory of that little girl, yet I do not recall the event itself, only her telling of it.

Since it is Friday, the rest of the family must work; so my mother and I drive around the city, hunting out the places I long to see. We stop at the Public Gardens and walk for a while. The peacock cages are gone. "They got rid of those years ago," my mother says, surprised that I am looking for them. "Of course," I say, "I remember now. They weren't here the last time I came either."

The Convent School across the street has also changed. The high, wrought iron fence has disappeared, as have the somber figures in long black habits who once paced the borders of their cloister clicking off prayers on trailing strings of rosary beads. A handful of women come and go through the main entrance, but nothing identifies them as nuns. Ten years ago they exchanged their habits for regular clothes; now they come and go as they please. I stand at the sidewalk, staring at the familiar red brick building, straining to recall the *feeling* of this place, how it was during my five years there — the hushed corridors, the spartan, disciplined life, the sense of journey. But the feeling will not come. In my study fifteen hundred miles away it came in great nostalgic waves.

"Halifax has really changed since you lived here," my mother says. "People are more prosperous. There are lots of things to do and see." This is true. I remember a stolid, grey city, muffled by blue laws. Now I find it charming, lively — a city I wouldn't mind living in. Why, then, do I feel this odd disappointment?

Over the weekend there is a good deal of visiting with my family, and I become absorbed in my sister's herb garden, the large workshed my brother is building, my mother's poetry group. I am a tourist in their lives now, admiring the views. The present has power: it is exciting, engrossing, immediate. But the old things, too, have power; and it is for them I find myself searching.

"Do you remember when you told me the facts of life?" I ask Jeannette. We are making pies in her kitchen and this quiet sharing reminds me of a summer afternoon long ago. "How innocent we were!"

"I didn't tell *you*," she says, "*You* told *me*."

"But that can't be right. I remember . . ."

"Listen, that's not something I'd forget. I was the older one, supposed to know everything. It was humiliating to have to find out such an important thing from my little sister." She grins, and I feel my mouth drop open. I watch her fingers flute the edges of the pie crust. Could I somehow have revised history?

"You're right about the innocent part, though," she adds. "Imagine anyone being fourteen and fifteen *now* and knowing as little as we did then."

On Monday morning I return to the Convent School to visit my old mentor, the one who took a special interest in the bright but unruly scholarship girl, who guided her transformation through several difficult years. The summer before my last year there she was transferred to Vancouver, a loss I sorely felt. Now, I have learned, she is back in her old role of school principal.

Though I have prepared myself for the small shock of seeing her without the habit, I am still surprised by the tall woman dressed in a plain skirt and blouse who greets me. She is younger than I expected, only in her mid fifties.

"It's so good to see you again, Mother." I say.

"It's just 'Margaret' now," she smiles. "We don't go by 'Mother' anymore."

I want so much to tell her what I remember — her small encouragements, the subtle challenges to my spirit — for I have had more than twenty years to calculate her gifts to me. But it feels strange, relating such personal things to someone I barely recognize, and I find myself clothing her in an imaginary habit, focusing on her eyes, her familiar mouth.

"You gave me a little book once, one of those tiny pocket diaries with a half-page for each day. There was only enough room for a sentence or two in each space, so you suggested I write down something I learned each day. Do you remember?"

"No, I don't really. But it sounds like a grand idea."

"Then, when I'd come to see you — which was almost every day — you'd ask what I'd written and we'd talk about it. That helped me through some really hard times."

Watching her, I sense that what I describe is simply her normal way with students. What she remembers most is her old affection for me.

After I have shared my treasure-hoard of memories and offered my gratitude, the present and the more recent past seem to nudge away those distant things. We talk of my life now, the great changes in her life, the school, the religious order. No longer do we speak as student and teacher. She becomes like someone I might meet on a train or at a professional meeting — a woman I find interesting and enjoy getting to know. The visit stretches on through lunch (I treat her to a lobster roll at the Lord Nelson Coffee Shop), and well into the afternoon. Intermittently I call her "Mother"; each time she corrects me gently, "It's 'Margaret' now."

"I just can't seem to say it," I admit finally, as I am preparing to leave.

"Practice it out loud a few times," she says good-naturedly. "Mar-gar-et. Mar-gar-et." We both laugh.

"Perhaps I am afraid that in finding Margaret I will lose Mother Connolly," I say, suddenly seeing it.

"Oh you won't lose her. But that relationship can't go anywhere anymore. We have an opportunity for something new now."

The whole time I am in Halifax the air is charged with the same odd tension: past and present fading into each other, old things shifting, rearranging themselves. My mother, too, seems to feel it. Together we make a short excursion to Louisburg in Cape Breton. I have never seen this rebuilt French fortress, though several of my American friends have, and my wish to see it now is part curiosity and part the need to claim it as my own. On the way we pass through areas which hold pieces of my mother's past — Larry's River, Louisdale — villages where she was a young, rural schoolteacher, many years ago. With some encouragement, she talks about those days: when it was nothing to walk ten miles, even in winter, to go to a dance; when people traveled by steamer; when rural schoolteachers boarded at the houses of their students. It is a world I know of only through her.

On the way back my mother suggests a detour through a small village she has not revisited in over thirty years. "It's where I first met your father," she explains. There is very little to Pomquet Station: a cluster of houses along a dirt road, an old, boarded-up general store, some barren fields. "There used to be a railroad station, and there were more houses then," my mother says. We drive back and forth on the dusty road, looking for landmarks.

With the help of a local teenager we find the site of the one-room school house where my mother once taught. Only the foundation remains, now overgrown with wild rose and raspberry bushes. We walk along the edges while my mother explains the layout, where the potbellied stove stood, where the children put their coats. I am struck again by the persistence of the past, its hold, its richness. It has been over forty years since my mother stood at the school house door ringing the bell, yet every detail is still alive in her.

"Your father was manager of that store." My mother points to a dilapidated, abandoned building. "It was a co-op then. I came down one day to buy a package of blue-lined envelopes and there he was. I was very impressed with him. He had travelled, he wrote poems and articles that were published in the paper. He wasn't like the local boys and farm hands who tried to court me."

We are both silent for a while. My mother's face is wistful, full of remembering. I stare at the old store with its boarded-up windows and doors, trying to picture that small event so long ago that changed my mother's life, and without which I would never have been.

For the remaining hours it takes us to drive back to Halifax, my mother talks about her years with my father: the courtship, the romance, the high expectations, the disillusionment, my father's illnesses, the four babies. I have never heard my mother talk of those years in quite this way before, with this joy of remembering that transcends the sorrows.

"Have you ever regretted marrying Dad?"

"Heavens no! I would never have had you children otherwise!"

"But weren't we an awful burden? If you had stayed single you could have continued teaching, writing. You would have had a totally different life."

"That's the one thing I have never regretted; you children were and are the best part of my life!"

We cut across to the Eastern Shore and drive through dozens of picturesque fishing villages. The sky and sea are a hard, bright blue. I remember now that there were many such days.

Soon it is time to return to Virginia. On my last full day in Halifax, I realize with a burst of panic that much I have come to do remains undone: I have not walked the mile-long path to Saint Agnes school, where I walked each day from third to sixth grade, nor found my old prom dresses and diaries, nor stood in fog, nor gazed at the sunset in dreamy longing from my old bedroom window — how is it I have forgotten these things? I rush upstairs to the window, but instead of the horizon, all I see is the leafy green of the trees in front of the house — trees once small and frail, whose great branches now crowd the sky. I open the closet door, but find only the things I brought with me, along with a few of my mother's winter clothes. There is a low cupboard in the room, a storage cubicle built into the front eave of the house, where I used to keep my treasures. Surely bits of the past still wait there, ready to disclose themselves.

I stoop before the door, but something in me hesitates. I recall the apple tree, the small book that changed my life, the shifting, slippery, selectiveness of memory. There is no retrieving the past. That fixed, solid whole does not exist; it is an invention. Invisible circuitries transform one thing into another and another; tracks grow over, cover themselves. I touch the small plywood door with the palm of my hand, and then I get up. Let whatever lies there keep its own secrets.

About the Author

Simone Poirier-Bures was born and raised in an Acadian family in Halifax, Nova Scotia. She is the author of *Candyman*, a novel set in Halifax, and *That Shining Place*, a memoir of Greece (winner of the 1996 Evelyn Richardson Award). Her stories and essays have been published widely in Canada, the United States, and Australia. She now lives in Virginia and teaches writing at Virginia Polytechnic Institute and State University, in Blacksburg, Virginia.

On *Candyman*:

"Evocatively written and gently paced, *Candyman* is like a chance encounter with an old friend: warm, welcome and nostalgic . . . "
— Kathleen Ratliff, *Roanoke Times & World News*

"Poirier-Bures displays a high level of craftsmanship, but more importantly, she is skilled at depicting intense and complex emotions without becoming melodramatic. For me, *Candyman* lingers on in memory like the true history of a family."
— Virgina Beaton, *The Mail Star*

On *That Shining Place*:

"This is a gentle memoir, wise and warm, bringing back the smells of oregano, the details of relationships."
— *The Ottawa Citizen*

"Reading *That Shining Place* makes this reviewer want to visit Crete. . . . Her stories, in this delightful memoir . . . are enchanting."
— *The Canadian Book Review Annual*